Albert Savarus

Honore de Balzac

Translated by Ellen Marriage

Contents

ALBERT SAVARUS

BY

Honore de Balzac

Translated by Ellen Marriage

Albert Savarus

by Honore de Balzac

Translated by Ellen Marriage

DEDICATION

To Madame Emile Girardin.

ALBERT SAVARUS

One of the few drawing-rooms where, under the Restoration, the Archbishop of Besancon was sometimes to be seen, was that of the Baronne de Watteville, to whom he was particularly attached on account of her religious sentiments.

A word as to this lady, the most important lady of Besancon.

Monsieur de Watteville, a descendant of the famous Watteville, the most successful and illustrious of murderers and renegades--his extraordinary adventures are too much a part of history to be related here--this nineteenth century Monsieur de Watteville was as gentle and peaceable as his ancestor of the **Grand Siecle** had been passionate and turbulent. After living in the **Comte** (La Franche Comte) like a wood-louse in the crack of a wainscot, he had married the heiress of the celebrated house of Rupt. Mademoiselle de Rupt brought twenty thousand francs a year in the funds to add to the ten thousand francs a year in real estate of the Baron de Watteville. The Swiss gentleman's coat-of-arms (the Wattevilles are Swiss) was then borne as an escutcheon of pretence on the old shield of the Rupts. The marriage, arranged in 1802, was solemnized in 1815 after the second Restoration. Within three years of the birth of a daughter all Madame de Watteville's grandparents were dead, and their estates wound up. Monsieur de Watteville's house was then sold, and they settled in the Rue de la Prefecture in the fine old mansion of the Rupts, with an immense garden stretching to the Rue du Perron. Madame de Watteville, devout as a girl, became even more so after her marriage. She is one of the queens of the saintly brotherhood which gives the upper circles of Besancon a solemn air and prudish manners in harmony with the character of the town.

Monsieur le Baron de Watteville, a dry, lean man devoid of intelligence, looked worn out without any one knowing whereby, for he enjoyed the profoundest ignorance; but as his wife was a red-haired woman, and of a stern nature that became proverbial (we still say "as sharp as Madame de Watteville"), some wits of the legal profession declared that he had been worn against that rock--**Rupt** is obviously derived from **rupes**. Scientific students of social phenomena will not fail to have observed that Rosalie was the only offspring of the union between the Wattevilles and the Rupts.

Monsieur de Watteville spent his existence in a handsome workshop with a lathe; he was a turner! As subsidiary to this pursuit, he took up a fancy for making collections. Philosophical doctors, devoted to the study of madness, regard this tendency towards collecting as a first degree of mental aberration when it is set on small things. The Baron de Watteville treasured shells and geological fragments of the neighborhood of Besancon. Some contradictory folk, especially women, would say of Monsieur de Watteville, "He has a noble soul! He perceived from the first days of his married life that he would never be his wife's master, so he threw himself into a mechanical occupation and good living."

The house of the Rupts was not devoid of a certain magnificence worthy of Louis XIV., and bore traces of the nobility of the two families who had mingled in 1815. The chandeliers of glass cut in the shape of leaves, the brocades, the damask, the carpets, the gilt furniture, were all in harmony with the old liveries and the old servants. Though served in blackened family plate, round a looking-glass tray furnished with Dresden china, the food was exquisite. The wines selected by Monsieur de Watteville, who, to occupy his time and vary his employments, was his own butler, enjoyed a sort of fame throughout the department. Madame de Watteville's fortune was a fine one; while her husband's, which consisted only of the estate of Rouxey, worth about ten thousand francs a year, was not increased by inheritance. It is needless to add that in consequence of Madame de Watteville's close intimacy with the Archbishop, the three or four clever or remarkable Abbes of the diocese who were not averse to good feeding were very much at home at her house.

At a ceremonial dinner given in honor of I know not whose wedding, at the beginning of September 1834, when the women were standing in a circle round the drawing-room fire, and the men in groups by the windows, every one exclaimed with pleasure at the entrance of Monsieur l'Abbe de Grancey, who was announced.

"Well, and the lawsuit?" they all cried.

"Won!" replied the Vicar-General. "The verdict of the Court, from which we had no hope, you know why----"

This was an allusion to the members of the First Court of Appeal of 1830; the Legitimists had almost all withdrawn.

"The verdict is in our favor on every point, and reverses the decision of the Lower Court."

"Everybody thought you were done for."

"And we should have been, but for me. I told our advocate to be off to Paris, and at the crucial moment I was able to secure a new pleader, to whom we owe our victory, a wonderful man--"

"At Besancon?" said Monsieur de Watteville, guilelessly.

"At Besancon," replied the Abbe de Grancey.

"Oh yes, Savaron," said a handsome young man sitting near the Baroness, and named de Soulas.

"He spent five or six nights over it; he devoured documents and briefs; he had seven or eight interviews of several hours with me," continued Monsieur de Grancey, who had just reappeared at the Hotel de Rupt for the first time in three weeks. "In short, Monsieur Savaron has just completely beaten the celebrated lawyer whom our adversaries had sent for from Paris. This young man is wonderful, the bigwigs say. Thus the chapter is twice victorious; it has triumphed in law and also

in politics, since it has vanquished Liberalism in the person of the
Counsel of our Municipality.--'Our adversaries,' so our advocate said,
'must not expect to find readiness on all sides to ruin the
Archbishoprics.'--The President was obliged to enforce silence. All
the townsfolk of Besancon applauded. Thus the possession of the
buildings of the old convent remains with the Chapter of the Cathedral
of Besancon. Monsieur Savaron, however, invited his Parisian opponent
to dine with him as they came out of court. He accepted, saying,
'Honor to every conqueror,' and complimented him on his success
without bitterness."

"And where did you unearth this lawyer?" said Madame de Watteville. "I
never heard his name before."

"Why, you can see his windows from hence," replied the Vicar-General.
"Monsieur Savaron lives in the Rue du Perron; the garden of his house
joins on to yours."

"But he is not a native of the Comte," said Monsieur de Watteville.

"So little is he a native of any place, that no one knows where he
comes from," said Madame de Chavoncourt.

"But who is he?" asked Madame de Watteville, taking the Abbe's arm to
go into the dining-room. "If he is a stranger, by what chance has he
settled at Besancon? It is a strange fancy for a barrister."

"Very strange!" echoed Amedee de Soulas, whose biography is here
necessary to the understanding of this tale.

In all ages France and England have carried on an exchange of trifles, which is all the more constant because it evades the tyranny of the Custom-house. The fashion that is called English in Paris is called French in London, and this is reciprocal. The hostility of the two nations is suspended on two points--the uses of words and the fashions of dress. ***God Save the King***, the national air of England, is a tune written by Lulli for the Chorus of Esther or of Athalie. Hoops, introduced at Paris by an Englishwoman, were invented in London, it is known why, by a Frenchwoman, the notorious Duchess of Portsmouth. They were at first so jeered at that the first Englishwoman who appeared in them at the Tuileries narrowly escaped being crushed by the crowd; but they were adopted. This fashion tyrannized over the ladies of Europe for half a century. At the peace of 1815, for a year, the long waists of the English were a standing jest; all Paris went to see Pothier and Brunet in ***Les Anglaises pour rire***; but in 1816 and 1817 the belt of the Frenchwoman, which in 1814 cut her across the bosom, gradually descended till it reached the hips.

Within ten years England has made two little gifts to our language. The ***Incroyable***, the ***Merveilleux***, the ***Elegant***, the three successes of the ***petit-maitre*** of discreditable etymology, have made way for the "dandy" and the "lion." The ***lion*** is not the parent of the ***lionne***. The ***lionne*** is due to the famous song by Alfred de Musset:

  Avez vou vu dans Barcelone

  . . . . .

  C'est ma maitresse et ma lionne.

There has been a fusion--or, if you prefer it, a confusion--of the two words and the leading ideas. When an absurdity can amuse Paris, which devours as many masterpieces as absurdities, the provinces can hardly be deprived of them. So, as soon as the ***lion*** paraded Paris with his mane, his beard and moustaches, his waistcoats and his eyeglass, maintained in its place, without the help of his hands, by the contraction of his cheek, and eye-socket, the chief towns of some departments had their sub-lions, who protested by the smartness of their trouser-straps against the untidiness of their fellow-townsmen.

Thus, in 1834, Besancon could boast of a *lion*, in the person of Monsieur Amedee-Sylvain de Soulas, spelt Souleyas at the time of the Spanish occupation. Amedee de Soulas is perhaps the only man in Besancon descended from a Spanish family. Spain sent men to manage her business in the Comte, but very few Spaniards settled there. The Soulas remained in consequence of their connection with Cardinal Granvelle. Young Monsieur de Soulas was always talking of leaving Besancon, a dull town, church-going, and not literary, a military centre and garrison town, of which the manners and customs and physiognomy are worth describing. This opinion allowed of his lodging, like a man uncertain of the future, in three very scantily furnished rooms at the end of the Rue Neuve, just where it opens into the Rue de la Prefecture.

Young Monsieur de Soulas could not possibly live without a tiger. This tiger was the son of one of his farmers, a small servant aged fourteen, thick-set, and named Babylas. The lion dressed his tiger very smartly--a short tunic-coat of iron-gray cloth, belted with patent leather, bright blue plush breeches, a red waistcoat, polished leather top-boots, a shiny hat with black lacing, and brass buttons with the arms of Soulas. Amedee gave this boy white cotton gloves and his washing, and thirty-six francs a month to keep himself--a sum that seemed enormous to the grisettes of Besancon: four hundred and twenty francs a year to a child of fifteen, without counting extras! The extras consisted in the price for which he could sell his turned clothes, a present when Soulas exchanged one of his horses, and the perquisite of the manure. The two horses, treated with sordid economy, cost, one with another, eight hundred francs a year. His bills for articles received from Paris, such as perfumery, cravats, jewelry, patent blacking, and clothes, ran to another twelve hundred francs. Add to this the groom, or tiger, the horses, a very superior style of dress, and six hundred francs a year for rent, and you will see a grand total of three thousand francs.

Now, Monsieur de Soulas' father had left him only four thousand francs a year, the income from some cottage farms which lent painful uncertainty to the rents. The lion had hardly three francs a day left for food, amusements, and gambling. He very often dined out, and breakfasted with remarkable frugality. When he was positively obliged to dine at his own cost, he sent his tiger to fetch a couple of dishes from a cookshop, never spending more than twenty-five sous.

Young Monsieur de Soulas was supposed to be a spendthrift, recklessly extravagant, whereas the poor man made the two ends meet in the year with a keenness and skill which would have done honor to a thrifty housewife. At Besancon in those days no one knew how great a tax on a man's capital were six francs spent in polish to spread on his boots or shoes, yellow gloves at fifty sous a pair, cleaned in the deepest secrecy to make them three times renewed, cravats costing ten francs, and lasting three months, four waistcoats at twenty-five francs, and trousers fitting close to the boots. How could he do otherwise, since we see women in Paris bestowing their special attention on simpletons who visit them, and cut out the most remarkable men by means of these frivolous advantages, which a man can buy for fifteen louis, and get his hair curled and a fine linen shirt into the bargain?

If this unhappy youth should seem to you to have become a *lion* on very cheap terms, you must know that Amedee de Soulas had been three times to Switzerland, by coach and in short stages, twice to Paris, and once from Paris to England. He passed as a well-informed traveler, and could say, "In England, where I went . . ." The dowagers of the

town would say to him, "You, who have been in England . . ." He had
been as far as Lombardy, and seen the shores of the Italian lakes. He
read new books. Finally, when he was cleaning his gloves, the tiger
Babylas replied to callers, "Monsieur is very busy." An attempt had
been made to withdraw Monsieur Amedee de Soulas from circulation by
pronouncing him "A man of advanced ideas." Amedee had the gift of
uttering with the gravity of a native the commonplaces that were in
fashion, which gave him the credit of being one of the most
enlightened of the nobility. His person was garnished with fashionable
trinkets, and his head furnished with ideas hall-marked by the press.

In 1834 Amedee was a young man of five-and-twenty, of medium height,
dark, with a very prominent thorax, well-made shoulders, rather plump
legs, feet already fat, white dimpled hands, a beard under his chin,
moustaches worthy of the garrison, a good-natured, fat, rubicund face,
a flat nose, and brown expressionless eyes; nothing Spanish about him.
He was progressing rapidly in the direction of obesity, which would be
fatal to his pretensions. His nails were well kept, his beard trimmed,
the smallest details of his dress attended to with English precision.
Hence Amedee de Soulas was looked upon as the finest man in Besancon.
A hairdresser who waited upon him at a fixed hour--another luxury,
costing sixty francs a year--held him up as the sovereign authority in
matters of fashion and elegance.

Amedee slept late, dressed and went out towards noon, to go to one of
his farms and practise pistol-shooting. He attached as much importance
to this exercise as Lord Byron did in his later days. Then, at three
o'clock he came home, admired on horseback by the grisettes and the
ladies who happened to be at their windows. After an affectation of
study or business, which seemed to engage him till four, he dressed to
dine out, spent the evening in the drawing-rooms of the aristocracy of
Besancon playing whist, and went home to bed at eleven. No life could
be more above board, more prudent, or more irreproachable, for he

punctually attended the services at church on Sundays and holy days.

To enable you to understand how exceptional is such a life, it is necessary to devote a few words to an account of Besancon. No town ever offered more deaf and dumb resistance to progress. At Besancon the officials, the employes, the military, in short, every one engaged in governing it, sent thither from Paris to fill a post of any kind, are all spoken of by the expressive general name of ***the Colony***. The colony is neutral ground, the only ground where, as in church, the upper rank and the townsfolk of the place can meet. Here, fired by a word, a look, or gesture, are started those feuds between house and house, between a woman of rank and a citizen's wife, which endure till death, and widen the impassable gulf which parts the two classes of society. With the exception of the Clermont-Mont-Saint-Jean, the Beauffremont, the de Scey, and the Gramont families, with a few others who come only to stay on their estates in the Comte, the aristocracy of Besancon dates no further back than a couple of centuries, the time of the conquest by Louis XIV. This little world is essentially of the ***parlement***, and arrogant, stiff, solemn, uncompromising, haughty beyond all comparison, even with the Court of Vienna, for in this the nobility of Besancon would put the Viennese drawing-rooms to shame. As to Victor Hugo, Nodier, Fourier, the glories of the town, they are never mentioned, no one thinks about them. The marriages in these families are arranged in the cradle, so rigidly are the greatest things settled as well as the smallest. No stranger, no intruder, ever finds his way into one of these houses, and to obtain an introduction for the colonels or officers of title belonging to the first families in France when quartered there, requires efforts of diplomacy which Prince Talleyrand would gladly have mastered to use at a congress.

In 1834 Amedee was the only man in Besancon who wore trouser-straps; this will account for the young man's being regarded as a lion. And a little anecdote will enable you to understand the city of Besancon.

Some time before the opening of this story, the need arose at the prefecture for bringing an editor from Paris for the official newspaper, to enable it to hold its own against the little *Gazette*, dropped at Besancon by the great *Gazette*, and the *Patriot*, which frisked in the hands of the Republicans. Paris sent them a young man, knowing nothing about la Franche Comte, who began by writing them a leading article of the school of the *Charivari*. The chief of the moderate party, a member of the municipal council, sent for the journalist and said to him, "You must understand, monsieur, that we are serious, more than serious--tiresome; we resent being amused, and are furious at having been made to laugh. Be as hard of digestion as the toughest disquisitions in the Revue des Deux Mondes, and you will hardly reach the level of Besancon."

The editor took the hint, and thenceforth spoke the most incomprehensible philosophical lingo. His success was complete.

If young Monsieur de Soulas did not fall in the esteem of Besancon society, it was out of pure vanity on its part; the aristocracy were happy to affect a modern air, and to be able to show any Parisians of rank who visited the Comte a young man who bore some likeness to them.

All this hidden labor, all this dust thrown in people's eyes, this display of folly and latent prudence, had an object, or the *lion* of Besancon would have been no son of the soil. Amedee wanted to achieve a good marriage by proving some day that his farms were not mortgaged, and that he had some savings. He wanted to be the talk of the town, to be the finest and best-dressed man there, in order to win first the attention, and then the hand, of Mademoiselle Rosalie de Watteville.

In 1830, at the time when young Monsieur de Soulas was setting up in business as a dandy, Rosalie was but fourteen. Hence, in 1834,

Mademoiselle de Watteville had reached the age when young persons are easily struck by the peculiarities which attracted the attention of the town to Amedee. There are so many **lions** who become **lions** out of self-interest and speculation. The Wattevilles, who for twelve years had been drawing an income of fifty thousand francs a year, did not spend more than four-and-twenty thousand francs a year, while receiving all the upper circle of Besancon every Monday and Friday. On Monday they gave a dinner, on Friday an evening party. Thus, in twelve years, what a sum must have accumulated from twenty-six thousand francs a year, saved and invested with the judgment that distinguishes those old families! It was very generally supposed that Madame de Watteville, thinking she had land enough, had placed her savings in the three per cents, in 1830. Rosalie's dowry would therefore, as the best informed opined, amount to about twenty thousand francs a year. So for the last five years Amedee had worked like a mole to get into the highest favor of the severe Baroness, while laying himself out to flatter Mademoiselle de Watteville's conceit.

Madame de Watteville was in the secret of the devices by which Amedee succeeded in keeping up his rank in Besancon, and esteemed him highly for it. Soulas had placed himself under her wing when she was thirty, and at that time had dared to admire her and make her his idol; he had got so far as to be allowed--he alone in the world--to pour out to her all the unseemly gossip which almost all very precise women love to hear, being authorized by their superior virtue to look into the gulf without falling, and into the devil's snares without being caught. Do you understand why the lion did not allow himself the very smallest intrigue? He lived a public life, in the street so to speak, on purpose to play the part of a lover sacrificed to duty by the Baroness, and to feast her mind with the sins she had forbidden to her senses. A man who is so privileged as to be allowed to pour light stories into the ear of a bigot is in her eyes a charming man. If this exemplary youth had better known the human heart, he might without risk have allowed himself some flirtations among the grisettes of Besancon who looked up to him as a king; his affairs might perhaps have been all the more hopeful with the strict and prudish Baroness. To Rosalie our Cato affected prodigality; he professed a life of elegance, showing her in perspective the splendid part played by a woman of fashion in Paris, whither he meant to go as Depute.

All these manoeuvres were crowned with complete success. In 1834 the mothers of the forty noble families composing the high society of Besancon quoted Monsieur Amedee de Soulas as the most charming young man in the town; no one would have dared to dispute his place as cock of the walk at the Hotel de Rupt, and all Besancon regarded him as Rosalie de Watteville's future husband. There had even been some exchange of ideas on the subject between the Baroness and Amedee, to which the Baron's apparent nonentity gave some certainty.

Mademoiselle de Watteville, to whom her enormous prospective fortune at that time lent considerable importance, had been brought up exclusively within the precincts of the Hotel de Rupt--which her mother rarely quitted, so devoted was she to her dear Archbishop--and severely repressed by an exclusively religious education, and by her mother's despotism, which held her rigidly to principles. Rosalie knew absolutely nothing. Is it knowledge to have learned geography from Guthrie, sacred history, ancient history, the history of France, and the four rules all passed through the sieve of an old Jesuit? Dancing and music were forbidden, as being more likely to corrupt life than to grace it. The Baroness taught her daughter every conceivable stitch in tapestry and women's work--plain sewing, embroidery, netting. At seventeen Rosalie had never read anything but the *Lettres edifiantes* and some works on heraldry. No newspaper had ever defiled her sight. She attended mass at the Cathedral every morning, taken there by her mother, came back to breakfast, did needlework after a little walk in the garden, and received visitors, sitting with the baroness until dinner-time. Then, after dinner, excepting on Mondays and Fridays, she accompanied Madame de Watteville to other houses to spend the evening, without being allowed to talk more than the maternal rule permitted.

At eighteen Mademoiselle de Watteville was a slight, thin girl with a flat figure, fair, colorless, and insignificant to the last degree. Her eyes, of a very light blue, borrowed beauty from their lashes, which, when downcast, threw a shadow on her cheeks. A few freckles marred the whiteness of her forehead, which was shapely enough. Her face was exactly like those of Albert Durer's saints, or those of the painters before Perugino; the same plump, though slender modeling, the same delicacy saddened by ecstasy, the same severe guilelessness. Everything about her, even to her attitude, was suggestive of those virgins, whose beauty is only revealed in its mystical radiance to the eyes of the studious connoisseur. She had fine hands though red, and a pretty foot, the foot of an aristocrat.

She habitually wore simple checked cotton dresses; but on Sundays and in the evening her mother allowed her silk. The cut of her frocks, made at Besancon, almost made her ugly, while her mother tried to borrow grace, beauty, and elegance from Paris fashions; for through Monsieur de Soulas she procured the smallest trifles of her dress from thence. Rosalie had never worn a pair of silk stockings or thin boots, but always cotton stockings and leather shoes. On high days she was dressed in a muslin frock, her hair plainly dressed, and had bronze kid shoes.

This education, and her own modest demeanor, hid in Rosalie a spirit of iron. Physiologists and profound observers will tell you, perhaps to your astonishment, that tempers, characteristics, wit, or genius reappear in families at long intervals, precisely like what are known as hereditary diseases. Thus talent, like the gout, sometimes skips over two generations. We have an illustrious example of this phenomenon in George Sand, in whom are resuscitated the force, the power, and the imaginative faculty of the Marechal de Saxe, whose natural granddaughter she is.

The decisive character and romantic daring of the famous Watteville had reappeared in the soul of his grand-niece, reinforced by the tenacity and pride of blood of the Rupts. But these qualities--or faults, if you will have it so--were as deeply buried in this young girlish soul, apparently so weak and yielding, as the seething lavas within a hill before it becomes a volcano. Madame de Watteville alone, perhaps, suspected this inheritance from two strains. She was so severe to her Rosalie, that she replied one day to the Archbishop, who blamed her for being too hard on the child, "Leave me to manage her, monseigneur. I know her! She has more than one Beelzebub in her skin!"

The Baroness kept all the keener watch over her daughter, because she considered her honor as a mother to be at stake. After all, she had nothing else to do. Clotilde de Rupt, at this time five-and-thirty, and as good as widowed, with a husband who turned egg-cups in every variety of wood, who set his mind on making wheels with six spokes out of iron-wood, and manufactured snuff-boxes for everyone of his acquaintance, flirted in strict propriety with Amedee de Soulas. When this young man was in the house, she alternately dismissed and recalled her daughter, and tried to detect symptoms of jealousy in that youthful soul, so as to have occasion to repress them. She imitated the police in its dealings with the republicans; but she labored in vain. Rosalie showed no symptoms of rebellion. Then the arid bigot accused her daughter of perfect insensibility. Rosalie knew her mother well enough to be sure that if she had thought young Monsieur de Soulas *nice*, she would have drawn down on herself a smart reproof. Thus, to all her mother's incitement she replied merely by such phrases as are wrongly called Jesuitical--wrongly, because the Jesuits were strong, and such reservations are the ***chevaux de frise*** behind which weakness takes refuge. Then the mother regarded the girl as a dissembler. If by mischance a spark of the true nature of the Wattevilles and the Rupts blazed out, the mother armed herself with the respect due from children to their parents to reduce Rosalie to passive obedience.

This covert battle was carried on in the most secret seclusion of domestic life, with closed doors. The Vicar-General, the dear Abbe Grancey, the friend of the late Archbishop, clever as he was in his capacity of the chief Father Confessor of the diocese, could not discover whether the struggle had stirred up some hatred between the mother and daughter, whether the mother were jealous in anticipation, or whether the court Amedee was paying to the girl through her mother had not overstepped its due limits. Being a friend of the family, neither mother nor daughter, confessed to him. Rosalie, a little too much harried, morally, about young de Soulas, could not abide him, to use a homely phrase, and when he spoke to her, trying to take her heart by surprise, she received him but coldly. This aversion, discerned only by her mother's eyes, was a constant subject of admonition.

"Rosalie, I cannot imagine why you affect such coldness towards Amedee. Is it because he is a friend of the family, and because we like him--your father and I?"

"Well, mamma," replied the poor child one day, "if I made him welcome, should I not be still more in the wrong?"

"What do you mean by that?" cried Madame de Watteville. "What is the meaning of such words? Your mother is unjust, no doubt, and according to you, would be so in any case! Never let such an answer pass your lips again to your mother--" and so forth.

This quarrel lasted three hours and three-quarters. Rosalie noted the time. Her mother, pale with fury, sent her to her room, where Rosalie pondered on the meaning of this scene without discovering it, so guileless was she. Thus young Monsieur de Soulas, who was supposed by every one to be very near the end he was aiming at, all neckcloths set, and by dint of pots of patent blacking--an end which required so much waxing of his moustaches, so many smart waistcoats, wore out so many horseshoes and stays--for he wore a leather vest, the stays of the *lion*--Amedee, I say, was further away than any chance comer, although he had on his side the worthy and noble Abbe de Grancey.

"Madame," said Monsieur de Soulas, addressing the Baroness, while waiting till his soup was cool enough to swallow, and affecting to give a romantic turn to his narrative, "one fine morning the mail-coach dropped at the Hotel National a gentleman from Paris, who, after seeking apartments, made up his mind in favor of the first floor in Mademoiselle Galard's house, Rue du Perron. Then the stranger went straight to the Mairie, and had himself registered as a resident with all political qualifications. Finally, he had his name entered on the list of the barristers to the Court, showing his title in due form, and he left his card on all his new colleagues, the Ministerial officials, the Councillors of the Court, and the members of the bench, with the name, 'ALBERT SAVARON.' "

"The name of Savaron is famous," said Mademoiselle de Watteville, who was strong in heraldic information. "The Savarons of Savarus are one of the oldest, noblest, and richest families in Belgium."

"He is a Frenchman, and no man's son," replied Amedee de Soulas. "If he wishes to bear the arms of the Savarons of Savarus, he must add a bar-sinister. There is no one left of the Brabant family but a

Mademoiselle de Savarus, a rich heiress, and unmarried."

"The bar-sinister is, of course, the badge of a bastard; but the bastard of a Comte de Savarus is noble," answered Rosalie.

"Enough, that will do, mademoiselle!" said the Baroness.

"You insisted on her learning heraldry," said Monsieur de Watteville, "and she knows it very well."

"Go on, I beg, Monsieur de Soulas."

"You may suppose that in a town where everything is classified, known, pigeon-holed, ticketed, and numbered, as in Besancon, Albert Savaron was received without hesitation by the lawyers of the town. They were satisfied to say, 'Here is a man who does not know his Besancon. Who the devil can have sent him here? What can he hope to do? Sending his card to the Judges instead of calling in person! What a blunder!' And so, three days after, Savaron had ceased to exist. He took as his servant old Monsieur Galard's man--Galard being dead--Jerome, who can cook a little. Albert Savaron was all the more completely forgotten, because no one had seen him or met him anywhere."

"Then, does he not go to mass?" asked Madame de Chavoncourt.

"He goes on Sundays to Saint-Pierre, but to the early service at eight in the morning. He rises every night between one and two in the morning, works till eight, has his breakfast, and then goes on working. He walks in his garden, going round fifty, or perhaps sixty times; then he goes in, dines, and goes to bed between six and seven."

"How did you learn all that?" Madame de Chavoncourt asked Monsieur de Soulas.

"In the first place, madame, I live in the Rue Neuve, at the corner of the Rue du Perron; I look out on the house where this mysterious personage lodges; then, of course, there are communications between my tiger and Jerome."

"And you gossip with Babylas?"

"What would you have me do out riding?"

"Well--and how was it that you engaged a stranger for your defence?" asked the Baroness, thus placing the conversation in the hands of the Vicar-General.

"The President of the Court played this pleader a trick by appointing him to defend at the Assizes a half-witted peasant accused of forgery. But Monsieur Savaron procured the poor man's acquittal by proving his innocence and showing that he had been a tool in the hands of the real culprits. Not only did his line of defence succeed, but it led to the arrest of two of the witnesses, who were proved guilty and condemned. His speech struck the Court and the jury. One of these, a merchant, placed a difficult case next day in the hands of Monsieur Savaron, and he won it. In the position in which we found ourselves, Monsieur Berryer finding it impossible to come to Besancon, Monsieur de Garcenault advised him to employ this Monsieur Albert Savaron, foretelling our success. As soon as I saw him and heard him, I felt faith in him, and I was not wrong."

"Is he then so extraordinary?" asked Madame de Chavoncourt.

"Certainly, madame," replied the Vicar-General.

"Well, tell us about it," said Madame de Watteville.

"The first time I saw him," said the Abbe de Grancey, "he received me in his outer room next the ante-room--old Galard's drawing-room--which he has had painted like old oak, and which I found entirely lined with law-books, arranged on shelves also painted as old oak. The painting and the books are the sole decoration of the room, for the furniture consists of an old writing table of carved wood, six old armchairs covered with tapestry, window curtains of gray stuff bordered with green, and a green carpet over the floor. The ante-room stove heats this library as well. As I waited there I did not picture my advocate as a young man. But this singular setting is in perfect harmony with his person; for Monsieur Savaron came out in a black merino dressing-gown tied with a red cord, red slippers, a red flannel waistcoat, and a red smoking-cap."

"The devil's colors!" exclaimed Madame de Watteville.

"Yes," said the Abbe; "but a magnificent head. Black hair already streaked with a little gray, hair like that of Saint Peter and Saint Paul in pictures, with thick shining curls, hair as stiff as horse-hair; a round white throat like a woman's; a splendid forehead, furrowed by the strong median line which great schemes, great thoughts, deep meditations stamp on a great man's brow; an olive complexion marbled with red, a square nose, eyes of flame, hollow cheeks, with two long lines, betraying much suffering, a mouth with a sardonic smile, and a small chin, narrow, and too short; crow's feet on his temples; deep-set eyes, moving in their sockets like burning balls; but, in spite of all these indications of a violently passionate nature, his manner was calm, deeply resigned, and his voice of penetrating sweetness, which surprised me in Court by its easy flow; a true orator's voice, now clear and appealing, sometimes insinuating, but a voice of thunder when needful, and lending itself to sarcasm to become incisive.

"Monsieur Albert Savaron is of middle height, neither stout nor thin. And his hands are those of a prelate.

"The second time I called on him he received me in his bed-room, adjoining the library, and smiled at my astonishment when I saw there a wretched chest of drawers, a shabby carpet, a camp-bed, and cotton window-curtains. He came out of his private room, to which no one is admitted, as Jerome informed me; the man did not go in, but merely knocked at the door.

"The third time he was breakfasting in his library on the most frugal fare; but on this occasion, as he had spent the night studying our documents, as I had my attorney with me, and as that worthy Monsieur Girardet is long-winded, I had leisure to study the stranger. He certainly is no ordinary man. There is more than one secret behind that face, at once so terrible and so gentle, patient and yet impatient, broad and yet hollow. I saw, too, that he stooped a little, like all men who have some heavy burden to bear."

"Why did so eloquent a man leave Paris? For what purpose did he come to Besancon?" asked pretty Madame de Chavoncourt. "Could no one tell him how little chance a stranger has of succeeding here? The good folks of Besancon will make use of him, but they will not allow him to make use of them. Why, having come, did he make so little effort that it needed a freak of the President's to bring him forward?"

"After carefully studying that fine head," said the Abbe, looking keenly at the lady who had interrupted him, in such a way as to suggest that there was something he would not tell, "and especially after hearing him this morning reply to one of the bigwigs of the Paris Bar, I believe that this man, who may be five-and-thirty, will by and by make a great sensation."

"Why should we discuss him? You have gained your action, and paid him," said Madame de Watteville, watching her daughter, who, all the time the Vicar-General had been speaking, seemed to hang on his lips.

The conversation changed, and no more was heard of Albert Savaron.

The portrait sketched by the cleverest of the Vicars-General of the diocese had all the greater charm for Rosalie because there was a romance behind it. For the first time in her life she had come across the marvelous, the exceptional, which smiles on every youthful imagination, and which curiosity, so eager at Rosalie's age, goes forth to meet half-way. What an ideal being was this Albert--gloomy, unhappy, eloquent, laborious, as compared by Mademoiselle de Watteville to that chubby fat Count, bursting with health, paying compliments, and talking of the fashions in the very face of the splendor of the old counts of Rupt. Amedee had cost her many quarrels and scoldings, and, indeed, she knew him only too well; while this Albert Savaron offered many enigmas to be solved.

"Albert Savaron de Savarus," she repeated to herself.

Now, to see him, to catch sight of him! This was the desire of the girl to whom desire was hitherto unknown. She pondered in her heart, in her fancy, in her brain, the least phrases used by the Abbe de Grancey, for all his words had told.

"A fine forehead!" said she to herself, looking at the head of every man seated at the table; "I do not see one fine one.--Monsieur de Soulas' is too prominent; Monsieur de Grancey's is fine, but he is seventy, and has no hair, it is impossible to see where his forehead ends."

"What is the matter, Rosalie; you are eating nothing?"

"I am not hungry, mamma," said she. "A prelate's hands----" she went on to herself. "I cannot remember our handsome Archbishop's hands, though he confirmed me."

Finally, in the midst of her coming and going in the labyrinth of her meditations, she remembered a lighted window she had seen from her bed, gleaming through the trees of the two adjoining gardens, when she had happened to wake in the night. . . . "Then that was his light!" thought she. "I might see him!--I will see him."

"Monsieur de Grancey, is the Chapter's lawsuit quite settled?" said Rosalie point-blank to the Vicar-General, during a moment of silence.

Madame de Watteville exchanged rapid glances with the Vicar-General.

"What can that matter to you, my dear child?" she said to Rosalie, with an affected sweetness which made her daughter cautious for the rest of her days.

"It might be carried to the Court of Appeal, but our adversaries will think twice about that," replied the Abbe.

"I never could have believed that Rosalie would think about a lawsuit all through a dinner," remarked Madame de Watteville.

"Nor I either," said Rosalie, in a dreamy way that made every one laugh. "But Monsieur de Grancey was so full of it, that I was interested."

The company rose from table and returned to the drawing-room. All through the evening Rosalie listened in case Albert Savaron should be mentioned again; but beyond the congratulations offered by each newcomer to the Abbe on having gained his suit, to which no one added any praise of the advocate, no more was said about it. Mademoiselle de Watteville impatiently looked forward to bedtime. She had promised herself to wake at between two and three in the morning, and to look at Albert's dressing-room windows. When the hour came, she felt almost pleasure in gazing at the glimmer from the lawyer's candles that shone through the trees, now almost bare of their leaves. By the help of the strong sight of a young girl, which curiosity seems to make longer, she saw Albert writing, and fancied she could distinguish the color of the furniture, which she thought was red. From the chimney above the roof rose a thick column of smoke.

"While all the world is sleeping, he is awake--like God!" thought she.

The education of girls brings with it such serious problems--for the future of a nation is in the mother--that the University of France long since set itself the task of having nothing to do with it. Here is one of these problems: Ought girls to be informed on all points? Ought their minds to be under restraint? It need not be said that the religious system is one of restraint. If you enlighten them, you make them demons before their time; if you keep them from thinking, you end in the sudden explosion so well shown by Moliere in the character of Agnes, and you leave this suppressed mind, so fresh and clear-seeing, as swift and as logical as that of a savage, at the mercy of an accident. This inevitable crisis was brought on in Mademoiselle de Watteville by the portrait which one of the most prudent Abbes of the Chapter of Besancon imprudently allowed himself to sketch at a dinner party.

Next morning, Mademoiselle de Watteville, while dressing, necessarily looked out at Albert Savaron walking in the garden adjoining that of the Hotel de Rupt.

"What would have become of me," thought she, "if he had lived anywhere else? Here I can, at any rate, see him.--What is he thinking about?"

Having seen this extraordinary man, though at a distance, the only man whose countenance stood forth in contrast with crowds of Besancon faces she had hitherto met with, Rosalie at once jumped at the idea of getting into his house, of ascertaining the reason of so much mystery, of hearing that eloquent voice, of winning a glance from those fine eyes. All this she set her heart on, but how could she achieve it?

All that day she drew her needle through her embroidery with the obtuse concentration of a girl who, like Agnes, seems to be thinking of nothing, but who is reflecting on things in general so deeply, that her artifice is unfailing. As a result of this profound meditation, Rosalie thought she would go to confession. Next morning, after Mass, she had a brief interview with the Abbe Giroud at Saint-Pierre, and managed so ingeniously that the hour of her confession was fixed for Sunday morning at half-past seven, before the eight o'clock Mass. She committed herself to a dozen fibs in order to find herself, just for once, in the church at the hour when the lawyer came to Mass. Then she was seized with an impulse of extreme affection for her father; she went to see him in his workroom, and asked him for all sorts of information on the art of turning, ending by advising him to turn larger pieces, columns. After persuading her father to set to work on some twisted pillars, one of the difficulties of the turner's art, she suggested that he should make use of a large heap of stones that lay in the middle of the garden to construct a sort of grotto on which he might erect a little temple or Belvedere in which his twisted pillars could be used and shown off to all the world.

At the climax of the pleasure the poor unoccupied man derived from this scheme, Rosalie said, as she kissed him, "Above all, do not tell mamma who gave you the notion; she would scold me."

"Do not be afraid!" replied Monsieur de Watteville, who groaned as bitterly as his daughter under the tyranny of the terrible descendant of the Rupts.

So Rosalie had a certain prospect of seeing ere long a charming observatory built, whence her eye would command the lawyer's private room. And there are men for whose sake young girls can carry out such masterstrokes of diplomacy, while, for the most part, like Albert Savaron, they know it not.

The Sunday so impatiently looked for arrived, and Rosalie dressed with such carefulness as made Mariette, the ladies'-maid, smile.

"It is the first time I ever knew mademoiselle to be so fidgety," said Mariette.

"It strikes me," said Rosalie, with a glance at Mariette, which brought poppies to her cheeks, "that you too are more particular on some days than on others."

As she went down the steps, across the courtyard, and through the gates, Rosalie's heart beat, as everybody's does in anticipation of a great event. Hitherto, she had never known what it was to walk in the streets; for a moment she had felt as though her mother must read her schemes on her brow, and forbid her going to confession, and she now felt new blood in her feet, she lifted them as though she trod on fire. She had, of course, arranged to be with her confessor at a quarter-past eight, telling her mother eight, so as to have about a quarter of an hour near Albert. She got to church before Mass, and after a short prayer, went to see if the Abbe Giroud were in his confessional, simply to pass the time; and she thus placed herself in such a way as to see Albert as he came into church.

The man must have been atrociously ugly who did not seem handsome to Mademoiselle de Watteville in the frame of mind produced by her curiosity. And Albert Savaron, who was really very striking, made all the more impression on Rosalie because his mien, his walk, his carriage, everything down to his clothing, had the indescribable stamp which can only be expressed by the word Mystery.

He came in. The church, till now gloomy, seemed to Rosalie to be illuminated. The girl was fascinated by his slow and solemn demeanor, as of a man who bears a world on his shoulders and whose deep gaze, whose very gestures, combine to express a devastating or absorbing thought. Rosalie now understood the Vicar-General's words in their fullest extent. Yes, those eyes of tawny brown, shot with golden lights, covered ardor which revealed itself in sudden flashes. Rosalie, with a recklessness which Mariette noted, stood in the lawyer's way, so as to exchange glances with him; and this glance turned her blood, for it seethed and boiled as though its warmth were doubled.

As soon as Albert had taken a seat, Mademoiselle de Watteville quickly found a place whence she could see him perfectly during all the time the Abbe might leave her. When Mariette said, "Here is Monsieur Giroud," it seemed to Rosalie that the interview had lasted no more than a few minutes. By the time she came out from the confessional, Mass was over. Albert had left the church.

"The Vicar-General was right," thought she. "*He* is unhappy. Why should this eagle--for he has the eyes of an eagle--swoop down on Besancon? Oh, I must know everything! But how?"

Under the smart of this new desire Rosalie set the stitches of her worsted-work with exquisite precision, and hid her meditations under a little innocent air, which shammed simplicity to deceive Madame de Watteville.

From that Sunday, when Mademoiselle de Watteville had met that look, or, if you please, received this baptism of fire--a fine expression of Napoleon's which may be well applied to love--she eagerly promoted the plan for the Belvedere.

"Mamma," said she one day when two columns were turned, "my father has taken a singular idea into his head; he is turning columns for a Belvedere he intends to erect on the heap of stones in the middle of the garden. Do you approve of it? It seems to me--"

"I approve of everything your father does," said Madame de Watteville drily, "and it is a wife's duty to submit to her husband even if she does not approve of his ideas. Why should I object to a thing which is of no importance in itself, if only it amuses Monsieur de Watteville?"

"Well, because from thence we shall see into Monsieur de Soulas' rooms, and Monsieur de Soulas will see us when we are there. Perhaps remarks may be made--"

"Do you presume, Rosalie, to guide your parents, and think you know more than they do of life and the proprieties?"

"I say no more, mamma. Besides, my father said that there would be a room in the grotto, where it would be cool, and where we can take coffee."

"Your father has had an excellent idea," said Madame de Watteville, who forthwith went to look at the columns.

She gave her entire approbation to the Baron de Watteville's design, while choosing for the erection of this monument a spot at the bottom of the garden, which could not be seen from Monsieur de Soulas' windows, but whence they could perfectly see into Albert Savaron's rooms. A builder was sent for, who undertook to construct a grotto, of which the top should be reached by a path three feet wide through the rock-work, where periwinkles would grow, iris, clematis, ivy, honeysuckle, and Virginia creeper. The Baroness desired that the inside should be lined with rustic wood-work, such as was then the fashion for flower-stands, with a looking-glass against the wall, an ottoman forming a box, and a table of inlaid bark. Monsieur de Soulas proposed that the floor should be of asphalt. Rosalie suggested a hanging chandelier of rustic wood.

"The Wattevilles are having something charming done in their garden," was rumored in Besancon.

"They are rich, and can afford a thousand crowns for a whim--"

"A thousand crowns!" exclaimed Madame de Chavoncourt.

"Yes, a thousand crowns," cried young Monsieur de Soulas. "A man has been sent for from Paris to rusticate the interior but it will be very pretty. Monsieur de Watteville himself is making the chandelier, and has begun to carve the wood."

"Berquet is to make a cellar under it," said an Abbe.

"No," replied young Monsieur de Soulas, "he is raising the kiosk on a concrete foundation, that it may not be damp."

"You know the very least things that are done in that house," said Madame de Chavoncourt sourly, as she looked at one of her great girls waiting to be married for a year past.

Mademoiselle de Watteville, with a little flush of pride in thinking of the success of her Belvedere, discerned in herself a vast superiority over every one about her. No one guessed that a little girl, supposed to be a witless goose, had simply made up her mind to get a closer view of the lawyer Savaron's private study.

Albert Savaron's brilliant defence of the Cathedral Chapter was all the sooner forgotten because the envy of the other lawyers was aroused. Also, Savaron, faithful to his seclusion, went nowhere. Having no friends to cry him up, and seeing no one, he increased the chances of being forgotten which are common to strangers in Besancon. Nevertheless, he pleaded three times at the Commercial Tribunal in three knotty cases which had to be carried to the superior Court. He thus gained as clients four of the chief merchants of the place, who discerned in him so much good sense and sound legal purview that they placed their claims in his hands.

On the day when the Watteville family inaugurated the Belvedere, Savaron also was founding a monument. Thanks to the connections he had obscurely formed among the upper class of merchants in Besancon, he was starting a fortnightly paper, called the ***Eastern Review***, with the help of forty shares of five hundred francs each, taken up by his first ten clients, on whom he had impressed the necessity for promoting the interests of Besancon, the town where the traffic should meet between Mulhouse and Lyons, and the chief centre between Mulhouse and Rhone.

To compete with Strasbourg, was it not needful that Besancon should become a focus of enlightenment as well as of trade? The leading questions relating to the interests of Eastern France could only be dealt with in a review. What a glorious task to rob Strasbourg and

Dijon of their literary importance, to bring light to the East of France, and compete with the centralizing influence of Paris! These reflections, put forward by Albert, were repeated by the ten merchants, who believed them to be their own.

Monsieur Savaron did not commit the blunder of putting his name in front; he left the finance of the concern to his chief client, Monsieur Boucher, connected by marriage with one of the great publishers of important ecclesiastical works; but he kept the editorship, with a share of the profits as founder. The commercial interest appealed to Dole, to Dijon, to Salins, to Neufchatel, to the Jura, Bourg, Nantua, Lous-le-Saulnier. The concurrence was invited of the learning and energy of every scientific student in the districts of le Bugey, la Bresse, and Franche Comte. By the influence of commercial interests and common feeling, five hundred subscribers were booked in consideration of the low price; the ***Review*** cost eight francs a quarter.

To avoid hurting the conceit of the provincials by refusing their articles, the lawyer hit on the good idea of suggesting a desire for the literary management of this ***Review*** to Monsieur Boucher's eldest son, a young man of two-and-twenty, very eager for fame, to whom the snares and woes of literary responsibilities were utterly unknown. Albert quietly kept the upper hand and made Alfred Boucher his devoted adherent. Alfred was the only man in Besancon with whom the king of the bar was on familiar terms. Alfred came in the morning to discuss the articles for the next number with Albert in the garden. It is needless to say that the trial number contained a "Meditation" by Alfred, which Savaron approved. In his conversations with Alfred, Albert would let drop some great ideas, subjects for articles of which Alfred availed himself. And thus the merchant's son fancied he was making capital out of the great man. To Alfred, Albert was a man of genius, of profound politics. The commercial world, enchanted at the success of the *Review*, had to pay up only three-tenths of their shares. Two hundred more subscribers, and the periodical would pay a dividend to the share-holders of five per cent, the editor remaining unpaid. This editing, indeed, was beyond price.

After the third number the *Review* was recognized for exchange by all the papers published in France, which Albert henceforth read at home. This third number included a tale signed "A. S.," and attributed to the famous lawyer. In spite of the small attention paid by the higher circle of Besancon to the *Review* which was accused of Liberal views, this, the first novel produced in the county, came under discussion that mid-winter at Madame de Chavoncourt's.

"Papa," said Rosalie, "a *Review* is published in Besancon; you ought to take it in; and keep it in your room, for mamma would not let me read it, but you will lend it to me."

Monsieur de Watteville, eager to obey his dear Rosalie, who for the last five months had given him so many proofs of filial affection,-- Monsieur de Watteville went in person to subscribe for a year to the *Eastern Review*, and lent the four numbers already out to his daughter. In the course of the night Rosalie devoured the tale--the first she had ever read in her life--but she had only known life for two months past. Hence the effect produced on her by this work must not be judged by ordinary rules. Without prejudice of any kind as to the greater or less merit of this composition from the pen of a Parisian who had thus imported into the province the manner, the brilliancy, if you will, of the new literary school, it could not fail to be a masterpiece to a young girl abandoning all her intelligence and her innocent heart to her first reading of this kind.

Also, from what she had heard said, Rosalie had by intuition conceived a notion of it which strangely enhanced the interest of this novel.

She hoped to find in it the sentiments, and perhaps something of the life of Albert. From the first pages this opinion took so strong a hold on her, that after reading the fragment to the end she was certain that it was no mistake. Here, then, is this confession, in which, according to the critics of Madame de Chavoncourt's drawing-room, Albert had imitated some modern writers who, for lack of inventiveness, relate their private joys, their private griefs, or the mysterious events of their own life.

*****

AMBITION FOR LOVE'S SAKE

In 1823 two young men, having agreed as a plan for a holiday to make a tour through Switzerland, set out from Lucerne one fine morning in the month of July in a boat pulled by three oarsmen. They started for Fluelen, intending to stop at every notable spot on the lake of the Four Cantons. The views which shut in the waters on the way from Lucerne to Fluelen offer every combination that the most exacting fancy can demand of mountains and rivers, lakes and rocks, brooks and pastures, trees and torrents. Here are austere solitudes and charming headlands, smiling and trimly kept meadows, forests crowning perpendicular granite cliffs, like plumes, deserted but verdant reaches opening out, and valleys whose beauty seems the lovelier in the dreamy distance.

As they passed the pretty hamlet of Gersau, one of the friends looked for a long time at a wooden house which seemed to have been recently built, enclosed by a paling, and standing on a promontory, almost bathed by the waters. As the boat rowed past, a woman's head was raised against the background of the room on the upper story of this house, to admire the effect of the boat on the lake. One of the young men met the glance thus indifferently given by the unknown fair.

"Let us stop here," said he to his friend. "We meant to make Lucerne our headquarters for seeing Switzerland; you will not take it amiss, Leopold, if I change my mind and stay here to take charge of our possessions. Then you can go where you please; my journey is ended. Pull to land, men, and put us out at this village; we will breakfast here. I will go back to Lucerne to fetch all our luggage, and before you leave you will know in which house I take a lodging, where you will find me on your return."

"Here or at Lucerne," replied Leopold, "the difference is not so great that I need hinder you from following your whim."

These two youths were friends in the truest sense of the word. They were of the same age; they had learned at the same school; and after studying the law, they were spending their holiday in the classical tour in Switzerland. Leopold, by his father's determination, was already pledged to a place in a notary's office in Paris. His spirit of rectitude, his gentleness, and the coolness of his senses and his brain, guaranteed him to be a docile pupil. Leopold could see himself a notary in Paris; his life lay before him like one of the highroads that cross the plains of France, and he looked along its whole length with philosophical resignation.

The character of his companion, whom we will call Rodolphe, presented a strong contrast with Leopold's, and their antagonism had no doubt had the result of tightening the bond that united them. Rodolphe was the natural son of a man of rank, who was carried off by a premature death before he could make any arrangements for securing the means of existence to a woman he fondly loved and to Rodolphe. Thus cheated by a stroke of fate, Rodolphe's mother had recourse to a heroic measure. She sold everything she owed to the munificence of her child's father for a sum of more than a hundred thousand francs, bought with it a life annuity for herself at a high rate, and thus acquired an income of about fifteen thousand francs, resolving to devote the whole of it to the education of her son, so as to give him all the personal advantages that might help to make his fortune, while saving, by strict economy, a small capital to be his when he came of age. It was bold; it was counting on her own life; but without this boldness the good mother would certainly have found it impossible to live and to bring her child up suitably, and he was her only hope, her future, the spring of all her joys.

Rodolphe, the son of a most charming Parisian woman, and a man of mark, a nobleman of Brabant, was cursed with extreme sensitiveness. From his infancy he had in everything shown a most ardent nature. In him mere desire became a guiding force and the motive power of his whole being, the stimulus to his imagination, the reason of his actions. Notwithstanding the pains taken by a clever mother, who was alarmed when she detected this predisposition, Rodolphe wished for things as a poet imagines, as a mathematician calculates, as a painter sketches, as a musician creates melodies. Tender-hearted, like his mother, he dashed with inconceivable violence and impetus of thought after the object of his desires; he annihilated time. While dreaming of the fulfilment of his schemes, he always overlooked the means of attainment. "When my son has children," said his other, "he will want them born grown up."

This fine frenzy, carefully directed, enabled Rodolphe to achieve his studies with brilliant results, and to become what the English call an accomplished gentleman. His mother was then proud of him, though still fearing a catastrophe if ever a passion should possess a heart at once so tender and so susceptible, so vehement and so kind. Therefore, the judicious mother had encouraged the friendship which bound Leopold to Rodolphe and Rodolphe to Leopold, since she saw in the cold and faithful young notary, a guardian, a comrade, who might to a certain extent take her place if by some misfortune she should be lost to her son. Rodolphe's mother, still handsome at three-and-forty, had inspired Leopold with an ardent passion. This circumstance made the two young men even more intimate.

So Leopold, knowing Rodolphe well, was not surprised to find him stopping at a village and giving up the projected journey to Saint-Gothard, on the strength of a single glance at the upper window of a house. While breakfast was prepared for them at the Swan Inn, the friends walked round the hamlet and came to the neighborhood of the pretty new house; here, while gazing about him and talking to the inhabitants, Rodolphe discovered the residence of some decent folk, who were willing to take him as a boarder, a very frequent custom in Switzerland. They offered him a bedroom looking over the lake and the mountains, and from whence he had a view of one of those immense sweeping reaches which, in this lake, are the admiration of every traveler. This house was divided by a roadway and a little creek from the new house, where Rodolphe had caught sight of the unknown fair one's face.

For a hundred francs a month Rodolphe was relieved of all thought for the necessaries of life. But, in consideration of the outlay the Stopfer couple expected to make, they bargained for three months' residence and a month's payment in advance. Rub a Swiss ever so little, and you find the usurer. After breakfast, Rodolphe at once made himself at home by depositing in his room such property as he had brought with him for the journey to the Saint-Gothard, and he watched Leopold as he set out, moved by the spirit of routine, to carry out the excursion for himself and his friend. When Rodolphe, sitting on a fallen rock on the shore, could no longer see Leopold's boat, he turned to examine the new house with stolen glances, hoping to see the fair unknown. Alas! he went in without its having given a sign of life. During dinner, in the company of Monsieur and Madame Stopfer, retired coopers from Neufchatel, he questioned them as to the neighborhood, and ended by learning all he wanted to know about the lady, thanks to his hosts' loquacity; for they were ready to pour out their budget of gossip without any pressing.

The fair stranger's name was Fanny Lovelace. This name (pronounced **Loveless**) is that of an old English family, but Richardson has given it to a creation whose fame eclipses all others! Miss Lovelace had come to settle by the lake for her father's health, the physicians having recommended him the air of Lucerne. These two English people had arrived with no other servant than a little girl of fourteen, a dumb child, much attached to Miss Fanny, on whom she waited very intelligently, and had settled, two winters since, with monsieur and Madame Bergmann, the retired head-gardeners of His Excellency Count Borromeo of Isola Bella and Isola Madre in the Lago Maggoire. These Swiss, who were possessed of an income of about a thousand crowns a year, had let the top story of their house to the Lovelaces for three years, at a rent of two hundred francs a year. Old Lovelace, a man of ninety, and much broken, was too poor to allow himself any gratifications, and very rarely went out; his daughter worked to maintain him, translating English books, and writing some herself, it was said. The Lovelaces could not afford to hire boats to row on the lake, or horses and guides to explore the neighborhood.

Poverty demanding such privation as this excites all the greater compassion among the Swiss, because it deprives them of a chance of profit. The cook of the establishment fed the three English boarders for a hundred francs a month inclusive. In Gersau it was generally believed, however, that the gardener and his wife, in spite of their pretensions, used the cook's name as a screen to net the little profits of this bargain. The Bergmanns had made beautiful gardens round their house, and had built a hothouse. The flowers, the fruit, and the botanical rarities of this spot were what had induced the

young lady to settle on it as she passed through Gersau. Miss Fanny
was said to be nineteen years old; she was the old man's youngest
child, and the object of his adulation. About two months ago she had
hired a piano from Lucerne, for she seemed to be crazy about music.

"She loves flowers and music, and she is unmarried!" thought Rodolphe;
"what good luck!"

The next day Rodolphe went to ask leave to visit the hothouses and
gardens, which were beginning to be somewhat famous. The permission
was not immediately granted. The retired gardeners asked, strangely
enough, to see Rodolphe's passport; it was sent to them at once. The
paper was not returned to him till next morning, by the hands of the
cook, who expressed her master's pleasure in showing him their place.
Rodolphe went to the Bergmanns', not without a certain trepidation,
known only to persons of strong feelings, who go through as much
passion in a moment as some men experience in a whole lifetime.

After dressing himself carefully to gratify the old gardeners of the
Borromean Islands, whom he regarded as the warders of his treasure, he
went all over the grounds, looking at the house now and again, but
with much caution; the old couple treated him with evident distrust.
But his attention was soon attracted by the little English deaf-mute,
in whom his discernment, though young as yet, enabled him to recognize
a girl of African, or at least of Sicilian, origin. The child had the
golden-brown color of a Havana cigar, eyes of fire, Armenian eyelids
with lashes of very un-British length, hair blacker than black; and
under this almost olive skin, sinews of extraordinary strength and
feverish alertness. She looked at Rodolphe with amazing curiosity and
effrontery, watching his every movement.

"To whom does that little Moresco belong?" he asked worthy Madame
Bergmann.

"To the English," Monsieur Bergmann replied.

"But she never was born in England!"

"They may have brought her from the Indies," said Madame Bergmann.

"I have been told that Miss Lovelace is fond of music. I should be delighted if, during my residence by the lake to which I am condemned by my doctor's orders, she would allow me to join her."

"They receive no one, and will not see anybody," said the old gardener.

Rodolphe bit his lips and went away, without having been invited into the house, or taken into the part of the garden that lay between the front of the house and the shore of the little promontory. On that side the house had a balcony above the first floor, made of wood, and covered by the roof, which projected deeply like the roof of a chalet on all four sides of the building, in the Swiss fashion. Rodolphe had loudly praised the elegance of this arrangement, and talked of the view from that balcony, but all in vain. When he had taken leave of the Bergmanns it struck him that he was a simpleton, like any man of spirit and imagination disappointed of the results of a plan which he had believed would succeed.

In the evening he, of course, went out in a boat on the lake, round and about the spit of land, to Brunnen and to Schwytz, and came in at nightfall. From afar he saw the window open and brightly lighted; he heard the sound of a piano and the tones of an exquisite voice. He made the boatman stop, and gave himself up to the pleasure of listening to an Italian air delightfully sung. When the singing ceased, Rodolphe landed and sent away the boat and rowers. At the cost of wetting his feet, he went to sit down under the water-worn granite shelf crowned by a thick hedge of thorny acacia, by the side of which ran a long lime avenue in the Bergmanns' garden. By the end of an hour he heard steps and voices just above him, but the words that reached his ears were all Italian, and spoken by two women.

He took advantage of the moment when the two speakers were at one end of the walk to slip noiselessly to the other. After half an hour of struggling he got to the end of the avenue, and there took up a position whence, without being seen or heard, he could watch the two women without being observed by them as they came towards him. What was Rodolphe's amazement on recognizing the deaf-mute as one of them; she was talking to Miss Lovelace in Italian.

It was now eleven o'clock at night. The stillness was so perfect on the lake and around the dwelling, that the two women must have thought themselves safe; in all Gersau there could be no eyes open but theirs. Rodolphe supposed that the girl's dumbness must be a necessary deception. From the way in which they both spoke Italian, Rodolphe suspected that it was the mother tongue of both girls, and concluded that the name of English also hid some disguise.

"They are Italian refugees," said he to himself, "outlaws in fear of the Austrian or Sardinian police. The young lady waits till it is dark to walk and talk in security."

He lay down by the side of the hedge, and crawled like a snake to find a way between two acacia shrubs. At the risk of leaving his coat behind him, or tearing deep scratches in his back, he got through the hedge when the so-called Miss Fanny and her pretended deaf-and-dumb maid were at the other end of the path; then, when they had come within twenty yards of him without seeing him, for he was in the shadow of the hedge, and the moon was shining brightly, he suddenly rose.

"Fear nothing," said he in French to the Italian girl, "I am not a spy. You are refugees, I have guessed that. I am a Frenchman whom one look from you has fixed at Gersau."

Rodolphe, startled by the acute pain caused by some steel instrument piercing his side, fell like a log.

"*Nel lago con pietra*!" said the terrible dumb girl.

"Oh, Gina!" exclaimed the Italian.

"She has missed me," said Rodolphe, pulling from his wound a stiletto, which had been turned by one of the false ribs. "But a little higher up it would have been deep in my heart.--I was wrong, Francesca," he went on, remembering the name he had heard little Gina repeat several times; "I owe her no grudge, do not scold her. The happiness of speaking to you is well worth the prick of a stiletto. Only show me the way out; I must get back to the Stopfer's house. Be easy; I shall tell nothing."

Francesca, recovering from her astonishment, helped Rodolphe to rise, and said a few words to Gina, whose eyes filled with tears. The two girls made him sit down on a bench and take off his coat, his waistcoat and cravat. Then Gina opened his shirt and sucked the wound strongly. Francesca, who had left them, returned with a large piece of sticking-plaster, which she applied to the wound.

"You can now walk as far as your house," she said.

Each took an arm, and Rodolphe was conducted to a side gate, of which the key was in Francesca's apron pocket.

"Does Gina speak French?" said Rodolphe to Francesca.

"No. But do not excite yourself," replied Francesca with some impatience.

"Let me look at you," said Rodolphe pathetically, "for it may be long before I am able to come again---"

He leaned against one of the gate-posts contemplating the beautiful Italian, who allowed him to gaze at her for a moment under the sweetest silence and the sweetest night which ever, perhaps, shone on this lake, the king of Swiss lakes.

Francesca was quite of the Italian type, and such as imagination supposes or pictures, or, if you will, dreams, that Italian women are. What first struck Rodolphe was the grace and elegance of a figure evidently powerful, though so slender as to appear fragile. An amber paleness overspread her face, betraying sudden interest, but it did not dim the voluptuous glance of her liquid eyes of velvety blackness. A pair of hands as beautiful as ever a Greek sculptor added to the polished arms of a statue grasped Rodolphe's arm, and their whiteness gleamed against his black coat. The rash Frenchman could but just discern the long, oval shape of her face, and a melancholy mouth showing brilliant teeth between the parted lips, full, fresh, and brightly red. The exquisite lines of this face guaranteed to Francesca permanent beauty; but what most struck Rodolphe was the adorable freedom, the Italian frankness of this woman, wholly absorbed as she was in her pity for him.

Francesca said a word to Gina, who gave Rodolphe her arm as far as the Stopfers' door, and fled like a swallow as soon as she had rung.

"These patriots do not play at killing!" said Rodolphe to himself as
he felt his sufferings when he found himself in his bed. " 'Nel
lago!' Gina would have pitched me into the lake with a stone tied to
my neck."

Next day he sent to Lucerne for the best surgeon there, and when he
came, enjoined on him absolute secrecy, giving him to understand that
his honor depended on it.

Leopold returned from his excursion on the day when his friend first
got out of bed. Rodolphe made up a story, and begged him to go to
Lucerne to fetch their luggage and letters. Leopold brought back the
most fatal, the most dreadful news: Rodolphe's mother was dead. While
the two friends were on their way from Bale to Lucerne, the fatal
letter, written by Leopold's father, had reached Lucerne the day they
left for Fluelen.

In spite of Leopold's utmost precautions, Rodolphe fell ill of a
nervous fever. As soon as Leopold saw his friend out of danger, he set
out for France with a power of attorney, and Rodolphe could thus
remain at Gersau, the only place in the world where his grief could
grow calmer. The young Frenchman's position, his despair, the
circumstances which made such a loss worse for him than for any other
man, were known, and secured him the pity and interest of every one in
Gersau. Every morning the pretended dumb girl came to see him and
bring him news of her mistress.

As soon as Rodolphe could go out he went to the Bergmanns' house, to
thank Miss Fanny Lovelace and her father for the interest they had
taken in his sorrow and his illness. For the first time since he had
lodged with the Bergmanns the old Italian admitted a stranger to his
room, where Rodolphe was received with the cordiality due to his
misfortunes and to his being a Frenchman, which excluded all distrust

of him. Francesca looked so lovely by candle-light that first evening that she shed a ray of brightness on his grieving heart. Her smiles flung the roses of hope on his woe. She sang, not indeed gay songs, but grave and solemn melodies suited to the state of Rodolphe's heart, and he observed this touching care.

At about eight o'clock the old man left the young people without any sign of uneasiness, and went to his room. When Francesca was tired of singing, she led Rodolphe on to the balcony, whence they perceived the sublime scenery of the lake, and signed to him to be seated by her on a rustic wooden bench.

"Am I very indiscreet in asking how old you are, cara Francesca?" said Rodolphe.

"Nineteen," said she, "well past."

"If anything in the world could soothe my sorrow," he went on, "it would be the hope of winning you from your father, whatever your fortune may be. So beautiful as you are, you seem to be richer than a prince's daughter. And I tremble as I confess to you the feelings with which you have inspired me; but they are deep--they are eternal."

"*Zitto*!" said Francesca, laying a finger of her right hand on her lips. "Say no more; I am not free. I have been married these three years."

For a few minutes utter silence reigned. When the Italian girl, alarmed at Rodolphe's stillness, went close to him, she found that he had fainted.

"*Povero*!" she said to herself. "And I thought him cold."

She fetched him some salts, and revived Rodolphe by making him smell at them.

"Married!" said Rodolphe, looking at Francesca. And then his tears flowed freely.

"Child!" said she. "But there is still hope. My husband is--"

"Eighty?" Rodolphe put in.

"No," said she with a smile, "but sixty-five. He has disguised himself as much older to mislead the police."

"Dearest," said Rodolphe, "a few more shocks of this kind and I shall die. Only when you have known me twenty years will you understand the strength and power of my heart, and the nature of its aspirations for happiness. This plant," he went on, pointing to the yellow jasmine which covered the balustrade, "does not climb more eagerly to spread itself in the sunbeams than I have clung to you for this month past. I love you with unique passion. That love will be the secret fount of my life--I may possibly die of it."

"Oh! Frenchman, Frenchman!" said she, emphasizing her exclamation with a little incredulous grimace.

"Shall I not be forced to wait, to accept you at the hands of time?" said he gravely. "But know this: if you are in earnest in what you have allowed to escape you, I will wait for you faithfully, without suffering any other attachment to grow up in my heart."

She looked at him doubtfully.

"None," said he, "not even a passing fancy. I have my fortune to make;

you must have a splendid one, nature created you a princess----"

At this word Francesca could not repress a faint smile, which gave her face the most bewildering expression, something subtle, like what the great Leonardo has so well depicted in the *Gioconda*. This smile made Rodolphe pause. "Ah yes!" he went on, "you must suffer much from the destitution to which exile has brought you. Oh, if you would make me happy above all men, and consecrate my love, you would treat me as a friend. Ought I not to be your friend?--My poor mother has left sixty thousand francs of savings; take half."

Francesca looked steadily at him. This piercing gaze went to the bottom of Rodolphe's soul.

"We want nothing; my work amply supplies our luxuries," she replied in a grave voice.

"And can I endure that a Francesca should work?" cried he. "One day you will return to your country and find all you left there." Again the Italian girl looked at Rodolphe. "And you will then repay me what you may have condescended to borrow," he added, with an expression full of delicate feeling.

"Let us drop the subject," said she, with incomparable dignity of gesture, expression, and attitude. "Make a splendid fortune, be one of the remarkable men of your country; that is my desire. Fame is a drawbridge which may serve to cross a deep gulf. Be ambitious if you must. I believe you have great and powerful talents, but use them rather for the happiness of mankind than to deserve me; you will be all the greater in my eyes."

In the course of this conversation, which lasted two hours, Rodolphe discovered that Francesca was an enthusiast for Liberal ideas, and for that worship of liberty which had led to the three revolutions in Naples, Piemont, and Spain. On leaving, he was shown to the door by Gina, the so-called mute. At eleven o'clock no one was astir in the village, there was no fear of listeners; Rodolphe took Gina into a corner, and asked her in a low voice and bad Italian, "Who are your master and mistress, child? Tell me, I will give you this fine new gold piece."

"Monsieur," said the girl, taking the coin, "my master is the famous bookseller Lamparini of Milan, one of the leaders of the revolution, and the conspirator of all others whom Austria would most like to have in the Spielberg."

"A bookseller's wife! Ah, so much the better," thought he; "we are on an equal footing.--And what is her family?" he added, "for she looks like a queen."

"All Italian women do," replied Gina proudly. "Her father's name is Colonna."

Emboldened by Francesca's modest rank, Rodolphe had an awning fitted to his boat and cushions in the stern. When this was done, the lover came to propose to Francesca to come out on the lake. The Italian accepted, no doubt to carry out her part of a young English Miss in the eyes of the villagers, but she brought Gina with her. Francesca Colonna's lightest actions betrayed a superior education and the highest social rank. By the way in which she took her place at the end of the boat Rodolphe felt himself in some sort cut off from her, and, in the face of a look of pride worthy of an aristocrat, the familiarity he had intended fell dead. By a glance Francesca made herself a princess, with all the prerogatives she might have enjoyed in the Middle Ages. She seemed to have read the thoughts of this vassal who was so audacious as to constitute himself her protector.

Already, in the furniture of the room where Francesca had received him, in her dress, and in the various trifles she made use of, Rodolphe had detected indications of a superior character and a fine fortune. All these observations now recurred to his mind; he became thoughtful after having been trampled on, as it were, by Francesca's dignity. Gina, her half-grown-up *confidante*, also seemed to have a mocking expression as she gave a covert or a side glance at Rodolphe. This obvious disagreement between the Italian lady's rank and her manners was a fresh puzzle to Rodolphe, who suspected some further trick like Gina's assumed dumbness.

"Where would you go, Signora Lamporani?" he asked.

"Towards Lucerne," replied Francesca in French.

"Good!" said Rodolphe to himself, "she is not startled by hearing me speak her name; she had, no doubt, foreseen that I should ask Gina-- she is so cunning.--What is your quarrel with me?" he went on, going at last to sit down by her side, and asking her by a gesture to give him her hand, which she withdrew. "You are cold and ceremonious; what, in colloquial language, we should call *short*."

"It is true," she replied with a smile. "I am wrong. It is not good manners; it is vulgar. In French you would call it inartistic. It is better to be frank than to harbor cold or hostile feelings towards a friend, and you have already proved yourself my friend. Perhaps I have gone too far with you. You must take me to be a very ordinary woman." --Rodolphe made many signs of denial.--"Yes," said the bookseller's wife, going on without noticing this pantomime, which, however, she plainly saw. "I have detected that, and naturally I have reconsidered my conduct. Well! I will put an end to everything by a few words of deep truth. Understand this, Rodolphe: I feel in myself the strength to stifle a feeling if it were not in harmony with my ideas or anticipation of what true love is. I could love--as we can love in Italy, but I know my duty. No intoxication can make me forget it. Married without my consent to that poor old man, I might take advantage of the liberty he so generously gives me; but three years of married life imply acceptance of its laws. Hence the most vehement passion would never make me utter, even involuntarily, a wish to find myself free.

"Emilio knows my character. He knows that without my heart, which is my own, and which I might give away, I should never allow anyone to take my hand. That is why I have just refused it to you. I desire to be loved and waited for with fidelity, nobleness, ardor, while all I can give is infinite tenderness of which the expression may not overstep the boundary of the heart, the permitted neutral ground. All this being thoroughly understood--Oh!" she went on with a girlish gesture, "I will be as coquettish, as gay, as glad, as a child which knows nothing of the dangers of familiarity."

This plain and frank declaration was made in a tone, an accent, and supported by a look which gave it the deepest stamp of truth.

"A Princess Colonna could not have spoken better," said Rodolphe, smiling.

"Is that," she answered with some haughtiness, "a reflection on the humbleness of my birth? Must your love flaunt a coat-of-arms? At Milan the noblest names are written over shop-doors: Sforza, Canova, Visconti, Trivulzio, Ursini; there are Archintos apothecaries; but, believe me, though I keep a shop, I have the feelings of a duchess."

"A reflection? Nay, madame, I meant it for praise."

"By a comparison?" she said archly.

"Ah, once for all," said he, "not to torture me if my words should ill express my feelings, understand that my love is perfect; it carries with it absolute obedience and respect."

She bowed as a woman satisfied, and said, "Then monsieur accepts the treaty?"

"Yes," said he. "I can understand that in a rich and powerful feminine nature the faculty of loving ought not to be wasted, and that you, out of delicacy, wished to restrain it. Ah! Francesca, at my age tenderness requited, and by so sublime, so royally beautiful a creature as you are--why, it is the fulfilment of all my wishes. To love you as you desire to be loved--is not that enough to make a young man guard himself against every evil folly? Is it not to concentrate all his powers in a noble passion, of which in the future he may be proud, and which can leave none but lovely memories? If you could but know with what hues you have clothed the chain of Pilatus, the Rigi, and this superb lake--"

"I want to know," said she, with the Italian artlessness which has always a touch of artfulness.

"Well, this hour will shine on all my life like a diamond on a queen's brow."

Francesca's only reply was to lay her hand on Rodolphe's.

"Oh dearest! for ever dearest!--Tell me, have you never loved?"

"Never."

"And you allow me to love you nobly, looking to heaven for the utmost fulfilment?" he asked.

She gently bent her head. Two large tears rolled down Rodolphe's cheeks.

"Why! what is the matter?" she cried, abandoning her imperial manner.

"I have now no mother whom I can tell of my happiness; she left this earth without seeing what would have mitigated her agony--"

"What?" said she.

"Her tenderness replaced by an equal tenderness----"

"*Povero mio*!" exclaimed the Italian, much touched. "Believe me," she went on after a pause, "it is a very sweet thing, and to a woman, a strong element of fidelity to know that she is all in all on earth to the man she loves; to find him lonely, with no family, with nothing in his heart but his love--in short, to have him wholly to herself."

When two lovers thus understand each other, the heart feels delicious peace, supreme tranquillity. Certainty is the basis for which human feelings crave, for it is never lacking to religious sentiment; man is always certain of being fully repaid by God. Love never believes itself secure but by this resemblance to divine love. And the raptures of that moment must have been fully felt to be understood; it is unique in life; it can never return no more, alas! than the emotions of youth. To believe in a woman, to make her your human religion, the fount of life, the secret luminary of all your least thoughts!--is not this a second birth? And a young man mingles with this love a little of the feeling he had for his mother.

Rodolphe and Francesca for some time remained in perfect silence, answering each other by sympathetic glances full of thoughts. They understood each other in the midst of one of the most beautiful scenes of Nature, whose glories, interpreted by the glory in their hearts, helped to stamp on their minds the most fugitive details of that unique hour. There had not been the slightest shade of frivolity in Francesca's conduct. It was noble, large, and without any second thought. This magnanimity struck Rodolphe greatly, for in it he recognized the difference between the Italian and the Frenchwoman. The waters, the land, the sky, the woman, all were grandiose and suave, even their love in the midst of this picture, so vast in its expanse, so rich in detail, where the sternness of the snowy peaks and their hard folds standing clearly out against the blue sky, reminded Rodolphe of the circumstances which limited his happiness; a lovely country shut in by snows.

This delightful intoxication of soul was destined to be disturbed. A boat was approaching from Lucerne; Gina, who had been watching it attentively, gave a joyful start, though faithful to her part as a mute. The bark came nearer; when at length Francesca could distinguish the faces on board, she exclaimed, "Tito!" as she perceived a young man. She stood up, and remained standing at the risk of being drowned. "Tito! Tito!" cried she, waving her handkerchief.

Tito desired the boatmen to slacken, and the two boats pulled side by side. The Italian and Tito talked with such extreme rapidity, and in a dialect unfamiliar to a man who hardly knew even the Italian of books, that Rodolphe could neither hear nor guess the drift of this conversation. But Tito's handsome face, Francesca's familiarity, and Gina's expression of delight, all aggrieved him. And indeed no lover can help being ill pleased at finding himself neglected for another, whoever he may be. Tito tossed a little leather bag to Gina, full of gold no doubt, and a packet of letters to Francesca, who began to read them, with a farewell wave of the hand to Tito.

"Get quickly back to Gersau," she said to the boatmen, "I will not let my poor Emilio pine ten minutes longer than he need."

"What has happened?" asked Rodolphe, as he saw Francesca finish reading the last letter.

"*La liberta*!" she exclaimed, with an artist's enthusiasm.

"*E denaro*!" added Gina, like an echo, for she had found her tongue.

"Yes," said Francesca, "no more poverty! For more than eleven months have I been working, and I was beginning to be tired of it. I am certainly not a literary woman."

"Who is this Tito?" asked Rodolphe.

"The Secretary of State to the financial department of the humble shop of the Colonnas, in other words, the son of our *ragionato*. Poor boy! he could not come by the Saint-Gothard, nor by the Mont-Cenis, nor by the Simplon; he came by sea, by Marseilles, and had to cross France. Well, in three weeks we shall be at Geneva, and living at our ease. Come, Rodolphe," she added, seeing sadness overspread the Parisian's face, "is not the Lake of Geneva quite as good as the Lake of Lucerne?"

"But allow me to bestow a regret on the Bergmanns' delightful house," said Rodolphe, pointing to the little promontory.

"Come and dine with us to add to your associations, *povero mio*," said she. "This is a great day; we are out of danger. My mother writes that within a year there will be an amnesty. Oh! *la cara patria*!"

These three words made Gina weep. "Another winter here," said she, "and I should have been dead!"

"Poor little Sicilian kid!" said Francesca, stroking Gina's head with an expression and an affection which made Rodolphe long to be so caressed, even if it were without love.

The boat grounded; Rodolphe sprang on to the sand, offered his hand to the Italian lady, escorted her to the door of the Bergmanns' house, and went to dress and return as soon as possible.

When he joined the librarian and his wife, who were sitting on the balcony, Rodolphe could scarcely repress an exclamation of surprise at seeing the prodigious change which the good news had produced in the old man. He now saw a man of about sixty, extremely well preserved, a lean Italian, as straight as an I, with hair still black, though thin and showing a white skull, with bright eyes, a full set of white teeth, a face like Caesar, and on his diplomatic lips a sardonic smile, the almost false smile under which a man of good breeding hides his real feelings.

"Here is my husband under his natural form," said Francesca gravely.

"He is quite a new acquaintance," replied Rodolphe, bewildered.

"Quite," said the librarian; "I have played many a part, and know well how to make up. Ah! I played one in Paris under the Empire, with Bourrienne, Madame Murat, Madame d'Abrantis *e tutte quanti*. Everything we take the trouble to learn in our youth, even the most futile, is of use. If my wife had not received a man's education--an unheard-of thing in Italy--I should have been obliged to chop wood to get my living here. *Povera* Francesca! who would have told me that she would some day maintain me!"

As he listened to this worthy bookseller, so easy, so affable, so hale, Rodolphe scented some mystification, and preserved the watchful silence of a man who has been duped.

"*Che avete, signor*?" Francesca asked with simplicity. "Does our happiness sadden you?"

"Your husband is a young man," he whispered in her ear.

She broke into such a frank, infectious laugh that Rodolphe was still more puzzled.

"He is but sixty-five, at your service," said she; "but I can assure you that even that is something--to be thankful for!"

"I do not like to hear you jest about an affection so sacred as this, of which you yourself prescribed the conditions."

"*Zitto*!" said she, stamping her foot, and looking whether her husband were listening. "Never disturb the peace of mind of that dear man, as simple as a child, and with whom I can do what I please. He is under my protection," she added. "If you could know with what generosity he risked his life and fortune because I was a Liberal! for he does not share my political opinions. Is not that love, Monsieur Frenchman?--But they are like that in his family. Emilio's younger brother was deserted for a handsome youth by the woman he loved. He thrust his sword through his own heart ten minutes after he had said to his servant, 'I could of course kill my rival, but that would grieve the *Diva* too deeply.' "

This mixture of dignity and banter, of haughtiness and playfulness,

made Francesca at this moment the most fascinating creature in the
world. The dinner and the evening were full of cheerfulness,
justified, indeed, by the relief of the two refugees, but depressing
to Rodolphe.

"Can she be fickle?" he asked himself as he returned to the Stopfers'
house. "She sympathized in my sorrow, and I cannot take part in her
joy!"

He blamed himself, justifying this girl-wife.

"She has no taint of hypocrisy, and is carried away by impulse,"
thought he, "and I want her to be like a Parisian woman."

Next day and the following days, in fact, for twenty days after,
Rodolphe spent all his time at the Bergmanns', watching Francesca
without having determined to watch her. In some souls admiration is
not independent of a certain penetration. The young Frenchman
discerned in Francesca the imprudence of girlhood, the true nature of
a woman as yet unbroken, sometimes struggling against her love, and at
other moments yielding and carried away by it. The old man certainly
behaved to her as a father to his daughter, and Francesca treated him
with a deeply felt gratitude which roused her instinctive nobleness.
The situation and the woman were to Rodolphe an impenetrable enigma,
of which the solution attracted him more and more.

These last days were full of secret joys, alternating with melancholy
moods, with tiffs and quarrels even more delightful than the hours
when Rodolphe and Francesca were of one mind. And he was more and more
fascinated by this tenderness apart from wit, always and in all things
the same, an affection that was jealous of mere nothings--already!

"You care very much for luxury?" said he one evening to Francesca, who was expressing her wish to get away from Gersau, where she missed many things.

"I!" cried she. "I love luxury as I love the arts, as I love a picture by Raphael, a fine horse, a beautiful day, or the Bay of Naples. Emilio," she went on, "have I ever complained here during our days of privation."

"You would not have been yourself if you had," replied the old man gravely.

"After all, is it not in the nature of plain folks to aspire to grandeur?" she asked, with a mischievous glance at Rodolphe and at her husband. "Were my feet made for fatigue?" she added, putting out two pretty little feet. "My hands"--and she held one out to Rodolphe-- "were those hands made to work?--Leave us," she said to her husband; "I want to speak to him."

The old man went into the drawing-room with sublime good faith; he was sure of his wife.

"I will not have you come with us to Geneva," she said to Rodolphe. "It is a gossiping town. Though I am far above the nonsense the world talks, I do not choose to be calumniated, not for my own sake, but for his. I make it my pride to be the glory of that old man, who is, after all, my only protector. We are leaving; stay here a few days. When you come on to Geneva, call first on my husband, and let him introduce you to me. Let us hide our great and unchangeable affection from the eyes of the world. I love you; you know it; but this is how I will prove it to you-- you shall never discern in my conduct anything whatever that may arouse your jealousy."

She drew him into a corner of the balcony, kissed him on the forehead, and fled, leaving him in amazement.

Next day Rodolphe heard that the lodgers at the Bergmanns' had left at daybreak. It then seemed to him intolerable to remain at Gersau, and he set out for Vevay by the longest route, starting sooner than was necessary. Attracted to the waters of the lake where the beautiful Italian awaited him, he reached Geneva by the end of October. To avoid the discomforts of the town he took rooms in a house at Eaux-Vives, outside the walls. As soon as he was settled, his first care was to ask his landlord, a retired jeweler, whether some Italian refugees from Milan had not lately come to reside at Geneva.

"Not so far as I know," replied the man. "Prince and Princess Colonna of Rome have taken Monsieur Jeanrenaud's place for three years; it is one of the finest on the lake. It is situated between the Villa Diodati and that of Monsieur Lafin-de-Dieu, let to the Vicomtesse de Beauseant. Prince Colonna has come to see his daughter and his son-in-law Prince Gandolphini, a Neopolitan, or if you like, a Sicilian, an old adherent of King Murat's, and a victim of the last revolution. These are the last arrivals at Geneva, and they are not Milanese. Serious steps had to be taken, and the Pope's interest in the Colonna family was invoked, to obtain permission from the foreign powers and the King of Naples for the Prince and Princess Gandolphini to live here. Geneva is anxious to do nothing to displease the Holy Alliance to which it owes its independence. *Our* part is not to ruffle foreign courts; there are many foreigners here, Russians and English."

"Even some Gevenese?"

"Yes, monsieur, our lake is so fine! Lord Byron lived here about seven years at the Villa Diodati, which every one goes to see now, like

Coppet and Ferney."

"You cannot tell me whether within a week or so a bookseller from Milan has come with his wife--named Lamporani, one of the leaders of the last revolution?"

"I could easily find out by going to the Foreigners' Club," said the jeweler.

Rodolphe's first walk was very naturally to the Villa Diodati, the residence of Lord Byron, whose recent death added to its attractiveness: for is not death the consecration of genius?

The road to Eaux-Vives follows the shore of the lake, and, like all the roads in Switzerland, is very narrow; in some spots, in consequence of the configuration of the hilly ground, there is scarcely space for two carriages to pass each other.

At a few yards from the Jeanrenauds' house, which he was approaching without knowing it, Rodolphe heard the sound of a carriage behind him, and, finding himself in a sunk road, he climbed to the top of a rock to leave the road free. Of course he looked at the approaching carriage--an elegant English phaeton, with a splendid pair of English horses. He felt quite dizzy as he beheld in this carriage Francesca, beautifully dressed, by the side of an old lady as hard as a cameo. A servant blazing with gold lace stood behind. Francesca recognized Rodolphe, and smiled at seeing him like a statue on a pedestal. The carriage, which the lover followed with his eyes as he climbed the hill, turned in at the gate of a country house, towards which he ran.

"Who lives here?" he asked the gardener.

"Prince and Princess Colonna, and Prince and Princess Gandolphini."

"Have they not just driven in?"

"Yes, sir."

In that instant a veil fell from Rodolphe's eyes; he saw clearly the meaning of the past.

"If only this is her last piece of trickery!" thought the thunder-struck lover to himself.

He trembled lest he should have been the plaything of a whim, for he had heard what a *capriccio* might mean in an Italian. But what a crime had he committed in the eyes of a woman--in accepting a born princess as a citizen's wife! in believing that a daughter of one of the most illustrious houses of the Middle Ages was the wife of a bookseller! The consciousness of his blunders increased Rodolphe's desire to know whether he would be ignored and repelled. He asked for Prince Gandolphini, sending in his card, and was immediately received by the false Lamparini, who came forward to meet him, welcomed him with the best possible grace, and took him to walk on a terrace whence there was a view of Geneva, the Jura, the hills covered with villas, and below them a wide expanse of the lake.

"My wife is faithful to the lakes, you see," he remarked, after pointing out the details to his visitor. "We have a sort of concert this evening," he added, as they returned to the splendid Villa Jeanrenaud. "I hope you will do me and the Princess the pleasure of seeing you. Two months of poverty endured in intimacy are equal to years of friendship."

Though he was consumed by curiosity, Rodolphe dared not ask to see the Princess; he slowly made his way back to Eaux-Vives, looking forward to the evening. In a few hours his passion, great as it had already been, was augmented by his anxiety and by suspense as to future events. He now understood the necessity for making himself famous, that he might some day find himself, socially speaking, on a level with his idol. In his eyes Francesca was made really great by the simplicity and ease of her conduct at Gersau. Princess Colonna's haughtiness, so evidently natural to her, alarmed Rodolphe, who would find enemies in Francesca's father and mother--at least so he might expect; and the secrecy which Princess Gandolphini had so strictly enjoined on him now struck him as a wonderful proof of affection. By not choosing to compromise the future, had she not confessed that she loved him?

At last nine o'clock struck; Rodolphe could get into a carriage and say with an emotion that is very intelligible, "To the Villa Jeanrenaud--to Prince Gandolphini's."

At last he saw Francesca, but without being seen by her. The Princess was standing quite near the piano. Her beautiful hair, so thick and long, was bound with a golden fillet. Her face, in the light of wax candles, had the brilliant pallor peculiar to Italians, and which looks its best only by artificial light. She was in full evening dress, showing her fascinating shoulders, the figure of a girl and the arms of an antique statue. Her sublime beauty was beyond all possible rivalry, though there were some charming women of Geneva, and other Italians, among them the dazzling and illustrious Princess Varese, and the famous singer Tinti, who was at that moment singing.

Rodolphe, leaning against the door-post, looked at the Princess, turning on her the fixed, tenacious, attracting gaze, charged with the full, insistent will which is concentrated in the feeling called desire, and thus assumes the nature of a vehement command. Did the flame of that gaze reach Francesca? Was Francesca expecting each instant to see Rodolphe? In a few minutes she stole a glance at the door, as though magnetized by this current of love, and her eyes, without reserve, looked deep into Rodolphe's. A slight thrill quivered through that superb face and beautiful body; the shock to her spirit reacted: Francesca blushed! Rodolphe felt a whole life in this exchange of looks, so swift that it can only be compared to a lightning flash. But to what could his happiness compare? He was loved. The lofty Princess, in the midst of her world, in this handsome villa, kept the pledge given by the disguised exile, the capricious beauty of Bergmanns' lodgings. The intoxication of such a moment enslaves a man for life! A faint smile, refined and subtle, candid and triumphant, curled Princess Gandolphini's lips, and at a moment when she did not feel herself observed she looked at Rodolphe with an expression which seemed to ask his pardon for having deceived him as to her rank.

When the song was ended Rodolphe could make his way to the Prince, who graciously led him to his wife. Rodolphe went through the ceremonial of a formal introduction to Princess and Prince Colonna, and to Francesca. When this was over, the Princess had to take part in the famous quartette, **_Mi manca la voce_**, which was sung by her with Tinti, with the famous tenor Genovese, and with a well-known Italian Prince then in exile, whose voice, if he had not been a Prince, would have made him one of the Princes of Art.

"Take that seat," said Francesca to Rodolphe, pointing to her own chair. "**_Oime_**! I think there is some mistake in my name; I have for the last minute been Princess Rodolphini."

It was said with the artless grace which revived, in this avowal hidden beneath a jest, the happy days at Gersau. Rodolphe reveled in the exquisite sensation of listening to the voice of the woman he adored, while sitting so close to her that one cheek was almost touched by the stuff of her dress and the gauze of her scarf. But when, at such a moment, ***Mi manca la voce*** is being sung, and by the finest voices in Italy, it is easy to understand what it was that brought the tears to Rodolphe's eyes.

In love, as perhaps in all else, there are certain circumstances, trivial in themselves, but the outcome of a thousand little previous incidents, of which the importance is immense, as an epitome of the past and as a link with the future. A hundred times already we have felt the preciousness of the one we love; but a trifle--the perfect touch of two souls united during a walk perhaps by a single word, by some unlooked-for proof of affection, will carry the feeling to its supremest pitch. In short, to express this truth by an image which has been pre-eminently successful from the earliest ages of the world, there are in a long chain points of attachment needed where the cohesion is stronger than in the intermediate loops of rings. This recognition between Rodolphe and Francesca, at this party, in the face of the world, was one of those intense moments which join the future to the past, and rivet a real attachment more deeply in the heart. It was perhaps of these incidental rivets that Bossuet spoke when he compared to them the rarity of happy moments in our lives--he who had such a living and secret experience of love.

Next to the pleasure of admiring the woman we love, comes that of seeing her admired by every one else. Rodolphe was enjoying both at once. Love is a treasury of memories, and though Rodolphe's was already full, he added to it pearls of great price; smiles shed aside for him alone, stolen glances, tones in her singing which Francesca addressed to him alone, but which made Tinti pale with jealousy, they were so much applauded. All his strength of desire, the special expression of his soul, was thrown over the beautiful Roman, who became unchangeably the beginning and the end of all his thoughts and actions. Rodolphe loved as every woman may dream of being loved, with

a force, a constancy, a tenacity, which made Francesca the very
substance of his heart; he felt her mingling with his blood as purer
blood, with his soul as a more perfect soul; she would henceforth
underlie the least efforts of his life as the golden sand of the
Mediterranean lies beneath the waves. In short, Rodolphe's lightest
aspiration was now a living hope.

At the end of a few days, Francesca understood this boundless love;
but it was so natural, and so perfectly shared by her, that it did not
surprise her. She was worthy of it.

"What is there that is strange?" said she to Rodolphe, as they walked
on the garden terrace, when he had been betrayed into one of those
outbursts of conceit which come so naturally to Frenchmen in the
expression of their feelings--"what is extraordinary in the fact of
your loving a young and beautiful woman, artist enough to be able to
earn her living like Tinti, and of giving you some of the pleasures of
vanity? What lout but would then become an Amadis? This is not in
question between you and me. What is needed is that we both love
faithfully, persistently; at a distance from each other for years,
with no satisfaction but that of knowing that we are loved."

"Alas!" said Rodolphe, "will you not consider my fidelity as devoid of
all merit when you see me absorbed in the efforts of devouring
ambition? Do you imagine that I can wish to see you one day exchange
the fine name of Gandolphini for that of a man who is a nobody? I want
to become one of the most remarkable men of my country, to be rich,
great--that you may be as proud of my name as of your own name of
Colonna."

"I should be grieved to see you without such sentiments in your
heart," she replied, with a bewitching smile. "But do not wear
yourself out too soon in your ambitious labors. Remain young. They say

that politics soon make a man old."

One of the rarest gifts in women is a certain gaiety which does not detract from tenderness. This combination of deep feeling with the lightness of youth added an enchanting grace at this moment to Francesca's charms. This is the key to her character; she laughs and she is touched; she becomes enthusiastic, and returns to arch raillery with a readiness, a facility, which makes her the charming and exquisite creature she is, and for which her reputation is known outside Italy. Under the graces of a woman she conceals vast learning, thanks to the excessively monotonous and almost monastic life she led in the castle of the old Colonnas.

This rich heiress was at first intended for the cloister, being the fourth child of Prince and Princess Colonna; but the death of her two brothers, and of her elder sister, suddenly brought her out of her retirement, and made her one of the most brilliant matches in the Papal States. Her elder sister had been betrothed to Prince Gandolphini, one of the richest landowners in Sicily; and Francesca was married to him instead, so that nothing might be changed in the position of the family. The Colonnas and Gandolphinis had always intermarried.

From the age of nine till she was sixteen, Francesca, under the direction of a Cardinal of the family, had read all through the library of the Colonnas, to make weight against her ardent imagination by studying science, art, and letters. But in these studies she acquired the taste for independence and liberal ideas, which threw her, with her husband, into the ranks of the revolution. Rodolphe had not yet learned that, besides five living languages, Francesca knew Greek, Latin, and Hebrew. The charming creature perfectly understood that, for a woman, the first condition of being learned is to keep it deeply hidden.

Rodolphe spent the whole winter at Geneva. This winter passed like a
day. When spring returned, notwithstanding the infinite delights of
the society of a clever woman, wonderfully well informed, young and
lovely, the lover went through cruel sufferings, endured indeed with
courage, but which were sometimes legible in his countenance, and
betrayed themselves in his manners or speech, perhaps because he
believed that Francesca shared them. Now and again it annoyed him to
admire her calmness. Like an Englishwoman, she seemed to pride herself
on expressing nothing in her face; its serenity defied love; he longed
to see her agitated; he accused her of having no feeling, for he
believed in the tradition which ascribes to Italian women a feverish
excitability.

"I am a Roman!" Francesca gravely replied one day when she took quite
seriously some banter on this subject from Rodolphe.

There was a depth of tone in her reply which gave it the appearance of
scathing irony, and which set Rodolphe's pulses throbbing. The month
of May spread before them the treasures of her fresh verdure; the sun
was sometimes as powerful as at midsummer. The two lovers happened to
be at a part of the terrace where the rock arises abruptly from the
lake, and were leaning over the stone parapet that crowns the wall
above a flight of steps leading down to a landing-stage. From the
neighboring villa, where there is a similar stairway, a boat presently
shot out like a swan, its flag flaming, its crimson awning spread over
a lovely woman comfortably reclining on red cushions, her hair
wreathed with real flowers; the boatman was a young man dressed like a
sailor, and rowing with all the more grace because he was under the
lady's eye.

"They are happy!" exclaimed Rodolphe, with bitter emphasis. "Claire de
Bourgogne, the last survivor of the only house which can ever vie with

the royal family of France--"

"Oh! of a bastard branch, and that a female line."

"At any rate, she is Vicomtesse de Beauseant; and she did not--"

"Did not hesitate, you would say, to bury herself here with Monsieur Gaston de Nueil, you would say," replied the daughter of the Colonnas. "She is only a Frenchwoman; I am an Italian, my dear sir!"

Francesca turned away from the parapet, leaving Rodolphe, and went to the further end of the terrace, whence there is a wide prospect of the lake. Watching her as she slowly walked away, Rodolphe suspected that he had wounded her soul, at once so simple and so wise, so proud and so humble. It turned him cold; he followed Francesca, who signed to him to leave her to herself. But he did not heed the warning, and detected her wiping away her tears. Tears! in so strong a nature.

"Francesca," said he, taking her hand, "is there a single regret in your heart?"

She was silent, disengaged her hand which held her embroidered handkerchief, and again dried her eyes.

"Forgive me!" he said. And with a rush, he kissed her eyes to wipe away the tears.

Francesca did not seem aware of his passionate impulse, she was so violently agitated. Rodolphe, thinking she consented, grew bolder; he put his arm round her, clasped her to his heart, and snatched a kiss. But she freed herself by a dignified movement of offended modesty, and, standing a yard off, she looked at him without anger, but with firm determination.

"Go this evening," she said. "We meet no more till we meet at Naples."

This order was stern, but it was obeyed, for it was Francesca's will.

On his return to Paris Rodolphe found in his rooms a portrait of Princess Gandolphini painted by Schinner, as Schinner can paint. The artist had passed through Geneva on his way to Italy. As he had positively refused to paint the portraits of several women, Rodolphe did not believe that the Prince, anxious as he was for a portrait of his wife, would be able to conquer the great painter's objections; but Francesca, no doubt, had bewitched him, and obtained from him--which was almost a miracle--an original portrait for Rodolphe, and a duplicate for Emilio. She told him this in a charming and delightful letter, in which the mind indemnified itself for the reserve required by the worship of the proprieties. The lover replied. Thus began, never to cease, a regular correspondence between Rodolphe and Francesca, the only indulgence they allowed themselves.

Rodolphe, possessed by an ambition sanctified by his love, set to work. First he longed to make his fortune, and risked his all in an undertaking to which he devoted all his faculties as well as his capital; but he, an inexperienced youth, had to contend against duplicity, which won the day. Thus three years were lost in a vast enterprise, three years of struggling and courage.

The Villele ministry fell just when Rodolphe was ruined. The valiant lover thought he would seek in politics what commercial industry had refused him; but before braving the storms of this career, he went, all wounded and sick at heart, to have his bruises healed and his courage revived at Naples, where the Prince and Princess had been

reinstated in their place and rights on the King's accession. This, in
the midst of his warfare, was a respite full of delights; he spent
three months at the Villa Gandolphini, rocked in hope.

Rodolphe then began again to construct his fortune. His talents were
already known; he was about to attain the desires of his ambition; a
high position was promised him as the reward of his zeal, his
devotion, and his past services, when the storm of July 1830 broke,
and again his bark was swamped.

She, and God! These are the only witnesses of the brave efforts, the
daring attempts of a young man gifted with fine qualities, but to
whom, so far, the protection of luck--the god of fools--has been
denied. And this indefatigable wrestler, upheld by love, comes back to
fresh struggles, lighted on his way by an always friendly eye, an ever
faithful heart.

Lovers! Pray for him!

*****

As she finished this narrative, Mademoiselle de Watteville's cheeks
were on fire; there was a fever in her blood. She was crying--but with
rage. This little novel, inspired by the literary style then in
fashion, was the first reading of the kind that Rosalie had ever had
the chance of devouring. Love was depicted in it, if not by a master-
hand, at any rate by a man who seemed to give his own impressions; and
truth, even if unskilled, could not fail to touch a virgin soul. Here
lay the secret of Rosalie's terrible agitation, of her fever and her
tears; she was jealous of Francesca Colonna.

She never for an instant doubted the sincerity of this poetical
flight; Albert had taken pleasure in telling the story of his passion,

while changing the names of persons and perhaps of places. Rosalie was possessed by infernal curiosity. What woman but would, like her, have wanted to know her rival's name--for she too loved! As she read these pages, to her really contagious, she had said solemnly to herself, "I love him!"--She loved Albert, and felt in her heart a gnawing desire to fight for him, to snatch him from this unknown rival. She reflected that she knew nothing of music, and that she was not beautiful.

"He will never love me!" thought she.

This conclusion aggravated her anxiety to know whether she might not be mistaken, whether Albert really loved an Italian Princess, and was loved by her. In the course of this fateful night, the power of swift decision, which had characterized the famous Watteville, was fully developed in his descendant. She devised those whimsical schemes, round which hovers the imagination of most young girls when, in the solitude to which some injudicious mothers confine them, they are roused by some tremendous event which the system of repression to which they are subjected could neither foresee nor prevent. She dreamed of descending by a ladder from the kiosk into the garden of the house occupied by Albert; of taking advantage of the lawyer's being asleep to look through the window into his private room. She thought of writing to him, or of bursting the fetters of Besancon society by introducing Albert to the drawing-room of the Hotel de Rupt. This enterprise, which to the Abbe de Grancey even would have seemed the climax of the impossible, was a mere passing thought.

"Ah!" said she to herself, "my father has a dispute pending as to his land at les Rouxey. I will go there! If there is no lawsuit, I will manage to make one, and *he* shall come into our drawing-room!" she cried, as she sprang out of bed and to the window to look at the fascinating gleam which shone through Albert's nights. The clock struck one; he was still asleep.

"I shall see him when he gets up; perhaps he will come to his window."

At this instant Mademoiselle de Watteville was witness to an incident which promised to place in her power the means of knowing Albert's secrets. By the light of the moon she saw a pair of arms stretched out from the kiosk to help Jerome, Albert's servant, to get across the coping of the wall and step into the little building. In Jerome's accomplice Rosalie at once recognized Mariette the lady's-maid.

"Mariette and Jerome!" said she to herself. "Mariette, such an ugly girl! Certainly they must be ashamed of themselves."

Though Mariette was horribly ugly and six-and-thirty, she had inherited several plots of land. She had been seventeen years with Madame de Watteville, who valued her highly for her bigotry, her honesty, and long service, and she had no doubt saved money and invested her wages and perquisites. Hence, earning about ten louis a year, she probably had by this time, including compound interest and her little inheritance, not less than ten thousand francs.

In Jerome's eyes ten thousand francs could alter the laws of optics; he saw in Mariette a neat figure; he did not perceive the pits and seams which virulent smallpox had left on her flat, parched face; to him the crooked mouth was straight; and ever since Savaron, by taking him into his service, had brought him so near to the Wattevilles' house, he had laid siege systematically to the maid, who was as prim and sanctimonious as her mistress, and who, like every ugly old maid, was far more exacting than the handsomest.

If the night-scene in the kiosk is thus fully accounted for to all perspicacious readers, it was not so to Rosalie, though she derived from it the most dangerous lesson that can be given, that of a bad

example. A mother brings her daughter up strictly, keeps her under her
wing for seventeen years, and then, in one hour, a servant girl
destroys the long and painful work, sometimes by a word, often indeed
by a gesture! Rosalie got into bed again, not without considering how
she might take advantage of her discovery.

Next morning, as she went to Mass accompanied by Mariette--her mother
was not well--Rosalie took the maid's arm, which surprised the country
wench not a little.

"Mariette," said she, "is Jerome in his master's confidence?"

"I do not know, mademoiselle."

"Do not play the innocent with me," said Mademoiselle de Watteville
drily. "You let him kiss you last night under the kiosk; I no longer
wonder that you so warmly approved of my mother's ideas for the
improvements she planned."

Rosalie could feel how Mariette was trembling by the shaking of her
arm.

"I wish you no ill," Rosalie went on. "Be quite easy; I shall not say
a word to my mother, and you can meet Jerome as often as you please."

"But, mademoiselle," said Mariette, "it is perfectly respectable;
Jerome honestly means to marry me--"

"But then," said Rosalie, "why meet at night?"

Mariette was dumfounded, and could make no reply.

"Listen, Mariette; I am in love too! In secret and without any return.

I am, after all, my father's and mother's only child. You have more to hope for from me than from any one else in the world--"

"Certainly, mademoiselle, and you may count on us for life or death," exclaimed Mariette, rejoiced at the unexpected turn of affairs.

"In the first place, silence for silence," said Rosalie. "I will not marry Monsieur de Soulas; but one thing I will have, and must have; my help and favor are yours on one condition only."

"What is that?"

"I must see the letters which Monsieur Savaron sends to the post by Jerome."

"But what for?" said Mariette in alarm.

"Oh! merely to read them, and you yourself shall post them afterwards. It will cause a little delay; that is all."

At this moment they went into church, and each of them, instead of reading the order of Mass, fell into her own train of thought.

"Dear, dear, how many sins are there in all that?" thought Mariette.

Rosalie, whose soul, brain, and heart were completely upset by reading the story, by this time regarded it as history, written for her rival. By dint of thinking of nothing else, like a child, she ended by believing that the *Eastern Review* was no doubt forwarded to Albert's lady-love.

"Oh!" said she to herself, her head buried in her hands in the attitude of a person lost in prayer; "oh! how can I get my father to look through the list of people to whom the *Review* is sent?"

After breakfast she took a turn in the garden with her father, coaxing and cajoling him, and brought him to the kiosk.

"Do you suppose, my dear little papa, that our *Review* is ever read abroad?"

"It is but just started--"

"Well, I will wager that it is."

"It is hardly possible."

"Just go and find out, and note the names of any subscribers out of France."

Two hours later Monsieur de Watteville said to his daughter:

"I was right; there is not one foreign subscriber as yet. They hope to get some at Neufchatel, at Berne, and at Geneva. One copy, is in fact, sent to Italy, but it is not paid for--to a Milanese lady at her country house at Belgirate, on Lago Maggiore.

"What is her name?"

"The Duchesse d'Argaiolo."

"Do you know her, papa?"

"I have heard about her. She was by birth a Princess Soderini, a Florentine, a very great lady, and quite as rich as her husband, who has one of the largest fortunes in Lombardy. Their villa on the Lago

Maggiore is one of the sights of Italy."

Two days after, Mariette placed the following letter in Mademoiselle de Watteville's hand:--

Albert Savaron to Leopold Hannequin.

"Yes, 'tis so, my dear friend; I am at Besancon, while you thought I was traveling. I would not tell you anything till success should begin, and now it is dawning. Yes, my dear Leopold, after so many abortive undertakings, over which I have shed the best of my blood, have wasted so many efforts, spent so much courage, I have made up my mind to do as you have done--to start on a beaten path, on the highroad, as the longest but the safest. I can see you jump with surprise in your lawyer's chair!

"But do not suppose that anything is changed in my personal life, of which you alone in the world know the secret, and that under the reservations *she* insists on. I did not tell you, my friend; but I was horribly weary of Paris. The outcome of the first enterprise, on which I had founded all my hopes, and which came to a bad end in consequence of the utter rascality of my two partners, who combined to cheat and fleece me--me, though everything was done by my energy--made me give up the pursuit of a fortune after the loss of three years of my life. One of these years was spent in the law courts, and perhaps I should have come worse out of the scrape if I had not been made to study law when I was twenty.

"I made up my mind to go into politics solely, to the end that I may some day find my name on a list for promotion to the Senate under the title of Comte Albert Savaron de Savarus, and so revive in France a good name now extinct in Belgium--though indeed I am neither legitimate nor legitimized."

"Ah! I knew it! He is of noble birth!" exclaimed Rosalie, dropping the letter.

"You know how conscientiously I studied, how faithful and useful I was as an obscure journalist, and how excellent a secretary to the statesman who, on his part, was true to me in 1829. Flung to the depths once more by the revolution of July just when my name was becoming known, at the very moment when, as Master of Appeals, I was about to find my place as a necessary wheel in the political machine, I committed the blunder of remaining faithful to the fallen, and fighting for them, without them. Oh! why was I but three-and-thirty, and why did I not apply to you to make me eligible? I concealed from you all my devotedness and my dangers. What would you have? I was full of faith. We should not have agreed.

"Ten months ago, when you saw me so gay and contented, writing my political articles, I was in despair; I foresaw my fate, at the age of thirty-seven, with two thousand francs for my whole fortune, without the smallest fame, just having failed in a noble undertaking, the founding, namely, of a daily paper answering only to a need of the future instead of appealing to the passions of the moment. I did not know which way to turn, and I felt my own value! I wandered about, gloomy and hurt, through the lonely places of Paris--Paris which had slipped through my fingers-- thinking of my crushed ambitions, but never giving them up. Oh, what frantic letters I wrote at that time to *her*, my second conscience, my other self! Sometimes I would say to myself, 'Why did I sketch so vast a programme of life? Why demand everything? Why not wait for happiness while devoting myself to some mechanical employment.'

"I then looked about me for some modest appointment by which I might live. I was about to get the editorship of a paper under a manager who did not know much about it, a man of wealth and ambition, when I took fright. 'Would *she* ever accept as her husband a man who had stooped so low?' I wondered.

"This reflection made me two-and-twenty again. But, oh, my dear Leopold, how the soul is worn by these perplexities! What must not the caged eagles suffer, and imprisoned lions!--They suffer what Napoleon suffered, not at Saint Helena, but on the Quay of the Tuileries, on the 10th of August, when he saw Louis XVI. defending himself so badly while he could have quelled the insurrection; as he actually did, on the same spot, a little later, in Vendemiaire. Well, my life has been a torment of that kind, extending over four years. How many a speech to the Chamber have I not delivered in the deserted alleys of the Bois de Boulogne! These wasted harangues have at any rate sharpened my tongue and accustomed my mind to formulate its ideas in words. And while I was undergoing this secret torture, you were getting married, you had paid for your business, you were made law-clerk to the Maire of your district, after gaining a cross for a wound at Saint-Merri.

"Now, listen. When I was a small boy and tortured cock-chafers, the poor insects had one form of struggle which used almost to put me in a fever. It was when I saw them making repeated efforts to fly but without getting away, though they could spread their wings. We used to say, 'They are marking time.' Now was this sympathy? Was it a vision of my own future?--Oh! to spread my wings and yet be unable to fly! That has been my predicament since that fine undertaking by which I was disgusted, but which has now made four families rich.

"At last, seven months ago, I determined to make myself a name at the Paris Bar, seeing how many vacancies had been left by the promotion of several lawyers to eminent positions. But when I remembered the rivalry I had seen among men of the press, and how difficult it is to achieve anything of any kind in Paris, the arena where so many champions meet, I came to a determination painful to myself, but certain in its results, and perhaps quicker than any other. In the course of our conversations you had given me a picture of the society of Besancon, of the impossibility for a stranger to get on there, to produce the smallest effect, to get into society, or to succeed in any way whatever. It was there that I determined to set up my flag, thinking, and rightly, that I should meet with no opposition, but find myself alone to canvass for the election. The people of the Comte will not meet the outsider? The outsider will meet them! They refuse to admit him to their drawing-rooms, he will never go there! He never shows himself anywhere, not even in the streets! But there is one class that elects the deputies--the commercial class. I am going especially to study commercial questions, with which I am already familiar; I will gain their lawsuits, I will effect compromises, I will be the greatest pleader in Besancon. By and by I will start a **Review**, in which I will defend the interests of the country, will create them, or preserve them, or resuscitate them. When I shall have won a sufficient number of votes, my name will come out of the urn. For a long time the unknown barrister will be treated with contempt, but some circumstance will arise to bring him to the front--some unpaid defence, or a case which no other pleader will undertake.

"Well, my dear Leopold, I packed up my books in eleven cases, I bought such law-books as might prove useful, and I sent everything off, furniture and all, by carrier to Besancon. I collected my diplomas, and I went to bid you good-bye. The mail coach dropped

me at Besancon, where, in three days' time, I chose a little set
of rooms looking out over some gardens. I sumptuously arranged the
mysterious private room where I spend my nights and days, and
where the portrait of my divinity reigns--of her to whom my life
is dedicate, who fills it wholly, who is the mainspring of my
efforts, the secret of my courage, the cause of my talents. Then,
as soon as the furniture and books had come, I engaged an
intelligent man-servant, and there I sat for five months like a
hibernating marmot.

"My name had, however, been entered on the list of lawyers in the
town. At last I was called one day to defend an unhappy wretch at
the Assizes, no doubt in order to hear me speak for once! One of
the most influential merchants of Besancon was on the jury; he had
a difficult task to fulfil; I did my utmost for the man, and my
success was absolute and complete. My client was innocent; I very
dramatically secured the arrest of the real criminals, who had
come forward as witnesses. In short, the Court and the public were
united in their admiration. I managed to save the examining
magistrate's pride by pointing out the impossibility of detecting
a plot so skilfully planned.

"Then I had to fight a case for my merchant, and won his suit. The
Cathedral Chapter next chose me to defend a tremendous action
against the town, which had been going on for four years; I won
that. Thus, after three trials, I had become the most famous
advocate of Franche-Comte.

"But I bury my life in the deepest mystery, and so hide my aims. I
have adopted habits which prevent my accepting any invitations. I
am only to be consulted between six and eight in the morning; I go
to bed after my dinner, and work at night. The Vicar-General, a
man of parts, and very influential, who placed the Chapter's case

in my hands after they had lost it in the lower Court, of course professed their gratitude. 'Monsieur,' said I, 'I will win your suit, but I want no fee; I want more' (start of alarm on the Abbe's part). 'You must know that I am a great loser by putting myself forward in antagonism to the town. I came here only to leave the place as deputy. I mean to engage only in commercial cases, because commercial men return the members; they will distrust me if I defend "the priests"--for to them you are simply priests. If I undertake your defence, it is because I was, in 1828, private secretary to such a Minister' (again a start of surprise on the part of my Abbe), 'and Master of Appeals, under the name of Albert de Savarus' (another start). 'I have remained faithful to monarchical opinions; but, as you have not the majority of votes in Besancon, I must gain votes among the citizens. So the fee I ask of you is the votes you may be able secretly to secure for me at the opportune moment. Let us each keep our own counsel, and I will defend, for nothing, every case to which a priest of this diocese may be a party. Not a word about my previous life, and we will be true to each other.'

"When he came to thank me afterwards, he gave me a note for five hundred francs, and said in my ear, 'The votes are a bargain all the same.'--I have in the course of five interviews made a friend, I think, of this Vicar-General.

"Now I am overwhelmed with business, and I undertake no cases but those brought to me by merchants, saying that commercial questions are my specialty. This line of conduct attaches business men to me, and allows me to make friends with influential persons. So all goes well. Within a few months I shall have found a house to purchase in Besancon, so as to secure a qualification. I count on your lending me the necessary capital for this investment. If I should die, if I should fail, the loss would be too small to be any consideration between you and me. You will get the interest out of the rental, and I shall take good care to look out for something cheap, so that you may lose nothing by this mortgage, which is indispensable.

"Oh! my dear Leopold, no gambler with the last remains of his fortune in his pocket, bent on staking it at the Cercle des Etrangers for the last time one night, when he must come away rich or ruined, ever felt such a perpetual ringing in his ears, such a nervous moisture on his palms, such a fevered tumult in his brain, such inward qualms in his body as I go through every day now that I am playing my last card in the game of ambition. Alas! my dear and only friend, for nearly ten years now I have been struggling. This battle with men and things, in which I have unceasingly poured out my strength and energy, and so constantly worn the springs of desire, has, so to speak, undermined my vitality. With all the appearance of a strong man of good health, I feel myself a wreck. Every day carries with it a shred of my inmost life. At every fresh effort I feel that I should never be able to begin again. I have no power, no vigor left but for happiness; and if it should never come to crown my head with roses, the *me* that is really me would cease to exist, I should be a ruined thing. I should wish for nothing more in the world. I should want to cease from living. You know that power and fame, the vast moral empire that I crave, is but secondary; it is to me only a means to happiness, the pedestal for my idol.

"To reach the goal and die, like the runner of antiquity! To see fortune and death stand on the threshold hand in hand! To win the beloved woman just when love is extinct! To lose the faculty of enjoyment after earning the right to be happy!--Of how many men has this been the fate!

"But there surely is a moment when Tantalus rebels, crosses his
arms, and defies hell, throwing up his part of the eternal dupe.
That is what I shall come to if anything should thwart my plan;
if, after stooping to the dust of provincial life, prowling like a
starving tiger round these tradesmen, these electors, to secure
their votes; if, after wrangling in these squalid cases, and
giving them my time--the time I might have spent on Lago Maggiore,
seeing the waters she sees, basking in her gaze, hearing her voice
--if, after all, I failed to scale the tribune and conquer the
glory that should surround the name that is to succeed to that of
Argaiolo! Nay, more than this, Leopold; there are days when I feel
a heady languor; deep disgust surges up from the depths of my
soul, especially when, abandoned to long day-dreams, I have lost
myself in anticipation of the joys of blissful love! May it not be
that our desire has only a certain modicum of power, and that it
perishes, perhaps, of a too lavish effusion of its essence? For,
after all, at this present, my life is fair, illuminated by faith,
work, and love.

"Farewell, my friend; I send love to your children, and beg you to
remember me to your excellent wife.--Yours,
"ALBERT."

Rosalie read this letter twice through, and its general purport was
stamped on her heart. She suddenly saw the whole of Albert's previous
existence, for her quick intelligence threw light on all the details,
and enabled her to take it all in. By adding this information to the
little novel published in the **Review**, she now fully understood
Albert. Of course, she exaggerated the greatness, remarkable as it
was, of this lofty soul and potent will, and her love for Albert
thenceforth became a passion, its violence enhanced by all the
strength of her youth, the weariness of her solitude, and the unspent

energy of her character. Love is in a young girl the effect of a
natural law; but when her craving for affection is centered in an
exceptional man, it is mingled with the enthusiasm which overflows in
a youthful heart. Thus Mademoiselle de Watteville had in a few days
reached a morbid and very dangerous stage of enamored infatuation. The
Baroness was much pleased with her daughter, who, being under the
spell of her absorbing thoughts, never resisted her will, seemed to be
devoted to feminine occupations, and realized her mother's ideal of a
docile daughter.

The lawyer was now engaged in Court two or three times a week. Though
he was overwhelmed with business, he found time to attend the trials,
call on the litigious merchants, and conduct the *Review*; keeping up
his personal mystery, from the conviction that the more covert and
hidden was his influence, the more real it would be. But he neglected
no means of success, reading up the list of electors of Besancon, and
finding out their interests, their characters, their various
friendships and antipathies. Did ever a Cardinal hoping to be made
Pope give himself more trouble?

One evening Mariette, on coming to dress Rosalie for an evening party,
handed to her, not without many groans over this treachery, a letter
of which the address made Mademoiselle de Watteville shiver and redden
and turn pale again as she read the address:

To Madame la Duchesse d'Argaiolo
(nee Princesse Soderini)
  At Belgirate,
    Lago Maggiore, Italy.

In her eyes this direction blazed as the words *Mene*, *Tekel*,
Upharsin, did in the eyes of Belshazzar. After concealing the
letter, Rosalie went downstairs to accompany her mother to Madame de

Chavoncourt's; and as long as the endless evening lasted, she was tormented by remorse and scruples. She had already felt shame at having violated the secrecy of Albert's letter to Leopold; she had several times asked herself whether, if he knew of her crime, infamous inasmuch as it necessarily goes unpunished, the high-minded Albert could esteem her. Her conscience answered an uncompromising "No."

She had expiated her sin by self-imposed penances; she fasted, she mortified herself by remaining on her knees, her arms outstretched for hours, and repeating prayers all the time. She had compelled Mariette to similar sets of repentance; her passion was mingled with genuine asceticism, and was all the more dangerous.

"Shall I read that letter, shall I not?" she asked herself, while listening to the Chavoncourt girls. One was sixteen, the other seventeen and a half. Rosalie looked upon her two friends as mere children because they were not secretly in love.--"If I read it," she finally decided, after hesitating for an hour between Yes and No, "it shall, at any rate, be the last. Since I have gone so far as to see what he wrote to his friend, why should I not know what he says to *her*? If it is a horrible crime, is it not a proof of love? Oh, Albert! am I not your wife?"

When Rosalie was in bed she opened the letter, dated from day to day, so as to give the Duchess a faithful picture of Albert's life and feelings.

"25th.

"My dear Soul, all is well. To my other conquests I have just added an invaluable one: I have done a service to one of the most influential men who work the elections. Like the critics, who make other men's reputations but can never make their own, he makes deputies though he never can become one. The worthy man wanted to show his gratitude without loosening his purse-strings by saying to me, 'Would you care to sit in the Chamber? I can get you returned as deputy.'

" 'If I ever make up my mind to enter on a political career,' replied I hypocritically, 'it would be to devote myself to the Comte, which I love, and where I am appreciated.'

" 'Well,' he said, 'we will persuade you, and through you we shall have weight in the Chamber, for you will distinguish yourself there.'

"And so, my beloved angel, say what you will, my perseverance will be rewarded. Ere long I shall, from the high place of the French Tribune, come before my country, before Europe. My name will be flung to you by the hundred voices of the French press.

"Yes, as you tell me, I was old when I came to Besancon, and Besancon has aged me more; but, like Sixtus V., I shall be young again the day after my election. I shall enter on my true life, my own sphere. Shall we not then stand in the same line? Count Savaron de Savarus, Ambassador I know not where, may surely marry a Princess Soderini, the widow of the Duc d'Argaiolo! Triumph restores the youth of men who have been preserved by incessant struggles. Oh, my Life! with what gladness did I fly from my library to my private room, to tell your portrait of this progress before writing to you! Yes, the votes I can command, those of the Vicar-General, of the persons I can oblige, and of this client, make my election already sure.

"26th.

"We have entered on the twelfth year since that blest evening when, by a look, the beautiful Duchess sealed the promises made by the exile Francesca. You, dear, are thirty-two, I am thirty-five; the dear Duke is seventy-seven--that is to say, ten years more than yours and mine put together, and he still keeps well! My patience is almost as great as my love, and indeed I need a few years yet to rise to the level of your name. As you see, I am in good spirits to-day, I can laugh; that is the effect of hope. Sadness or gladness, it all comes to me through you. The hope of success always carries me back to the day following that one on which I saw you for the first time, when my life became one with yours as the earth turns to the light. **Qual pianto** are these eleven years, for this is the 26th of December, the anniversary of my arrival at your villa on the Lake of Geneva. For eleven years have I been crying to you, while you shine like a star set too high for man to reach it.

"27th.

"No, dearest, do not go to Milan; stay at Belgirate. Milan terrifies me. I do not like that odious Milanese fashion of chatting at the Scala every evening with a dozen persons, among whom it is hard if no one says something sweet. To me solitude is like the lump of amber in whose heart an insect lives for ever in unchanging beauty. Thus the heart and soul of a woman remains pure and unaltered in the form of their first youth. Is it the **Tedeschi** that you regret?

"28th.

"Is your statue never to be finished? I should wish to have you in marble, in painting, in miniature, in every possible form, to beguile my impatience. I still am waiting for the view of Belgirate from the south, and that of the balcony; these are all that I now lack. I am so extremely busy that to-day I can only write you nothing--but that nothing is everything. Was it not of nothing that God made the world? That nothing is a word, God's word: I love you!

"30th.

"Ah! I have received your journal. Thanks for your punctuality.-- So you found great pleasure in seeing all the details of our first acquaintance thus set down? Alas! even while disguising them I was sorely afraid of offending you. We had no stories, and a *Review* without stories is a beauty without hair. Not being inventive by nature, and in sheer despair, I took the only poetry in my soul, the only adventure in my memory, and pitched it in the key in which it would bear telling; nor did I ever cease to think of you while writing the only literary production that will ever come from my heart, I cannot say from my pen. Did not the transformation of your fierce Sormano into Gina make you laugh?

"You ask after my health. Well, it is better than in Paris. Though I work enormously, the peacefulness of the surroundings has its effect on the mind. What really tries and ages me, dear angel, is the anguish of mortified vanity, the perpetual friction of Paris life, the struggle of rival ambitions. This peace is a balm.

"If you could imagine the pleasure your letter gives me!--the long, kind letter in which you tell me the most trivial incidents of your life. No! you women can never know to what a degree a true lover is interested in these trifles. It was an immense pleasure to see the pattern of your new dress. Can it be a matter of indifference to me to know what you wear? If your lofty brow is knit? If our writers amuse you? If Canalis' songs delight you? I read the books you read. Even to your boating on the lake every incident touched me. Your letter is as lovely, as sweet as your soul! Oh! flower of heaven, perpetually adored, could I have lived without those dear letters, which for eleven years have upheld me in my difficult path like a light, like a perfume, like a steady chant, like some divine nourishment, like everything which can soothe and comfort life.

"Do not fail me! If you knew what anxiety I suffer the day before they are due, or the pain a day's delay can give me! Is she ill? Is *he*? I am midway between hell and paradise.

"*O mia cara diva*, keep up your music, exercise your voice, practise. I am enchanted with the coincidence of employments and hours by which, though separated by the Alps, we live by precisely the same rule. The thought charms me and gives me courage. The first time I undertook to plead here--I forget to tell you this--I fancied that you were listening to me, and I suddenly felt the flash of inspiration which lifts the poet above mankind. If I am returned to the Chamber--oh! you must come to Paris to be present at my first appearance there!

"30th, Evening.

"Good heavens, how I love you! Alas! I have intrusted too much to my love and my hopes. An accident which should sink that

overloaded bark would end my life. For three years now I have not
seen you, and at the thought of going to Belgirate my heart beats
so wildly that I am forced to stop.--To see you, to hear that
girlish caressing voice! To embrace in my gaze that ivory skin,
glistening under the candlelight, and through which I can read
your noble mind! To admire your fingers playing on the keys, to
drink in your whole soul in a look, in the tone of an *Oime* or an
Alberto! To walk by the blossoming orange-trees, to live a few
months in the bosom of that glorious scenery!--That is life. What
folly it is to run after power, a name, fortune! But at Belgirate
there is everything; there is poetry, there is glory! I ought to
have made myself your steward, or, as that dear tyrant whom we
cannot hate proposed to me, live there as *cavaliere servente*,
only our passion was too fierce to allow of it.

"Farewell, my angel, forgive me my next fit of sadness in
consideration of this cheerful mood; it has come as a beam of
light from the torch of Hope, which has hitherto seemed to me a
Will-o'-the-wisp."

"How he loves her!" cried Rosalie, dropping the letter, which seemed
heavy in her hand. "After eleven years to write like this!"

"Mariette," said Mademoiselle de Watteville to her maid next morning,
"go and post this letter. Tell Jerome that I know all I wish to know,
and that he is to serve Monsieur Albert faithfully. We will confess
our sins, you and I, without saying to whom the letters belonged, nor
to whom they were going. I was in the wrong; I alone am guilty."

"Mademoiselle has been crying?" said Mariette.

"Yes, but I do not want that my mother should perceive it; give me
some very cold water."

In the midst of the storms of her passion Rosalie often listened to the voice of conscience. Touched by the beautiful fidelity of these two hearts, she had just said her prayers, telling herself that there was nothing left to her but to be resigned, and to respect the happiness of two beings worthy of each other, submissive to fate, looking to God for everything, without allowing themselves any criminal acts or wishes. She felt a better woman, and had a certain sense of satisfaction after coming to this resolution, inspired by the natural rectitude of youth. And she was confirmed in it by a girl's idea: She was sacrificing herself for *him*.

"She does not know how to love," thought she. "Ah! if it were I--I would give up everything to a man who loved me so.--To be loved!-- When, by whom shall I be loved? That little Monsieur de Soulas only loves my money; if I were poor, he would not even look at me."

"Rosalie, my child, what are you thinking about? You are working beyond the outline," said the Baroness to her daughter, who was making worsted-work slippers for the Baron.

Rosalie spent the winter of 1834-35 torn by secret tumults; but in the spring, in the month of April, when she reached the age of nineteen, she sometimes thought that it would be a fine thing to triumph over a Duchesse d'Argaiolo. In silence and solitude the prospect of this struggle had fanned her passion and her evil thoughts. She encouraged her romantic daring by making plan after plan. Although such characters are an exception, there are, unfortunately, too many Rosalies in the world, and this story contains a moral that ought to serve them as a warning.

In the course of this winter Albert de Savarus had quietly made considerable progress in Besancon. Confident of success, he now impatiently awaited the dissolution of the Chamber. Among the men of the moderate party he had won the suffrages of one of the makers of Besancon, a rich contractor, who had very wide influence.

Wherever they settled the Romans took immense pains, and spent enormous sums to have an unlimited supply of good water in every town of their empire. At Besancon they drank the water from Arcier, a hill at some considerable distance from Besancon. The town stands in a horseshoe circumscribed by the river Doubs. Thus, to restore an aqueduct in order to drink the same water that the Romans drank, in a town watered by the Doubs, is one of those absurdities which only succeed in a country place where the most exemplary gravity prevails. If this whim could be brought home to the hearts of the citizens, it would lead to considerable outlay; and this expenditure would benefit the influential contractor.

Albert Savaron de Savarus opined that the water of the river was good for nothing but to flow under the suspension bridge, and that the only drinkable water was that from Arcier. Articles were printed in the *Review* which merely expressed the views of the commercial interest of Besancon. The nobility and the citizens, the moderates and the legitimists, the government party and the opposition, everybody, in short, was agreed that they must drink the same water as the Romans, and boast of a suspension bridge. The question of the Arcier water was the order of the day at Besancon. At Besancon--as in the matter of the two railways to Versailles--as for every standing abuse--there were private interests unconfessed which gave vital force to this idea. The reasonable folk in opposition to this scheme, who were indeed but few, were regarded as old women. No one talked of anything but of Savaron's two projects. And thus, after eighteen months of underground labor, the ambitious lawyer had succeeded in stirring to its depths the most stagnant town in France, the most unyielding to foreign influence, in finding the length of its foot, to use a vulgar phrase, and exerting a preponderant influence without stirring from his own room. He had solved the singular problem of how to be powerful without being popular.

In the course of this winter he won seven lawsuits for various priests of Besancon. At moments he could breathe freely at the thought of his coming triumph. This intense desire, which made him work so many interests and devise so many springs, absorbed the last strength of his terribly overstrung soul. His disinterestedness was lauded, and he took his clients' fees without comment. But this disinterestedness was, in truth, moral usury; he counted on a reward far greater to him than all the gold in the world.

In the month of October 1834 he had brought, ostensibly to serve a merchant who was in difficulties, with money lent him by Leopold Hannequin, a house which gave him a qualification for election. He had not seemed to seek or desire this advantageous bargain.

"You are really a remarkable man," said the Abbe de Grancey, who, of course, had watched and understood the lawyer. The Vicar-General had come to introduce to him a Canon who needed his professional advice. "You are a priest who has taken the wrong turning." This observation struck Savarus.

Rosalie, on her part, had made up her mind, in her strong girl's head, to get Monsieur de Savarus into the drawing-room and acquainted with the society of the Hotel de Rupt. So far she had limited her desires to seeing and hearing Albert. She had compounded, so to speak, and a composition is often no more than a truce.

Les Rouxey, the inherited estate of the Wattevilles, was worth just ten thousand francs a year; but in other hands it would have yielded a great deal more. The Baron in his indifference--for his wife was to have, and in fact had, forty thousand francs a year--left the management of les Rouxey to a sort of factotum, an old servant of the Wattevilles named Modinier. Nevertheless, whenever the Baron and his wife wished to go out of the town, they went to les Rouxey, which is very picturesquely situated. The chateau and the park were, in fact, created by the famous Watteville, who in his active old age was passionately attached to this magnificent spot.

Between two precipitous hills--little peaks with bare summits known as the great and the little Rouxey--in the heart of a ravine where the torrents from the heights, with the Dent de Vilard at their head, come tumbling to join the lovely upper waters of the Doubs, Watteville had a huge dam constructed, leaving two cuttings for the overflow. Above this dam he made a beautiful lake, and below it two cascades; and these, uniting a few yards below the falls, formed a lovely little river to irrigate the barren, uncultivated valley, and these two hills he enclosed in a ring fence, and built himself a retreat on the dam, which he widened to two acres by accumulating above it all the soil which had to be removed to make a channel for the river and the irrigation canals.

When the Baron de Watteville thus obtained the lake above his dam he was owner of the two hills, but not of the upper valley thus flooded, through which there had been at all times a right-of-way to where it ends in a horseshoe under the Dent de Vilard. But this ferocious old man was so widely dreaded, that so long as he lived no claim was urged by the inhabitants of Riceys, the little village on the further side of the Dent de Vilard. When the Baron died, he left the slopes of the two Rouxey hills joined by a strong wall, to protect from inundation the two lateral valleys opening into the valley of Rouxey, to the right and left at the foot of the Dent de Vilard. Thus he died the master of the Dent de Vilard.

His heirs asserted their protectorate of the village of Riceys, and so maintained the usurpation. The old assassin, the old renegade, the old Abbe Watteville, ended his career by planting trees and making a fine road over the shoulder of one of the Rouxey hills to join the highroad. The estate belonging to this park and house was extensive, but badly cultivated; there were chalets on both hills and neglected forests of timber. It was all wild and deserted, left to the care of nature, abandoned to chance growths, but full of sublime and unexpected beauty. You may now imagine les Rouxey.

It is unnecessary to complicate this story by relating all the prodigious trouble and the inventiveness stamped with genius, by which Rosalie achieved her end without allowing it to be suspected. It is enough to say that it was in obedience to her mother that she left Besancon in the month of May 1835, in an antique traveling carriage drawn by a pair of sturdy hired horses, and accompanied her father to les Rouxey.

To a young girl love lurks in everything. When she rose, the morning after her arrival, Mademoiselle de Watteville saw from her bedroom window the fine expanse of water, from which the light mists rose like smoke, and were caught in the firs and larches, rolling up and along the hills till they reached the heights, and she gave a cry of admiration.

"They loved by the lakes! *She* lives by a lake! A lake is certainly full of love!" she thought.

A lake fed by snows has opalescent colors and a translucency that makes it one huge diamond; but when it is shut in like that of les Rouxey, between two granite masses covered with pines, when silence broods over it like that of the Savannas or the Steppes, then every one must exclaim as Rosalie did.

"We owe that," said her father, "to the notorious Watteville."

"On my word," said the girl, "he did his best to earn forgiveness. Let us go in a boat to the further end; it will give us an appetite for breakfast."

The Baron called two gardener lads who knew how to row, and took with him his prime minister Modinier. The lake was about six acres in breadth, in some places ten or twelve, and four hundred in length. Rosalie soon found herself at the upper end shut in by the Dent de Vilard, the Jungfrau of that little Switzerland.

"Here we are, Monsieur le Baron," said Modinier, signing to the gardeners to tie up the boat; "will you come and look?"

"Look at what?" asked Rosalie.

"Oh, nothing!" exclaimed the Baron. "But you are a sensible girl; we have some little secrets between us, and I may tell you what ruffles my mind. Some difficulties have arisen since 1830 between the village authorities of Riceys and me, on account of this very Dent de Vilard, and I want to settle the matter without your mother's knowing anything about it, for she is stubborn; she is capable of flinging fire and flames broadcast, particularly if she should hear that the Mayor of Riceys, a republican, got up this action as a sop to his people."

Rosalie had presence of mind enough to disguise her delight, so as to work more effectually on her father.

"What action?" said she.

"Mademoiselle, the people of Riceys," said Modinier, "have long enjoyed the right of grazing and cutting fodder on their side of the Dent de Vilard. Now Monsieur Chantonnit, the Maire since 1830, declares that the whole Dent belongs to his district, and maintains that a hundred years ago, or more, there was a way through our grounds. You understand that in that case we should no longer have them to ourselves. Then this barbarian would end by saying, what the old men in the village say, that the ground occupied by the lake was appropriated by the Abbe de Watteville. That would be the end of les Rouxey; what next?"

"Indeed, my child, between ourselves, it is the truth," said Monsieur de Watteville simply. "The land is an usurpation, with no title-deed but lapse of time. And, therefore, to avoid all worry, I should wish to come to a friendly understanding as to my border line on this side of the Dent de Vilard, and I will then raise a wall."

"If you give way to the municipality, it will swallow you up. You ought to have threatened Riceys."

"That is just what I told the master last evening," said Modinier. "But in confirmation of that view I proposed that he should come to see whether, on this side of the Dent or on the other, there may not be, high or low, some traces of an enclosure."

For a century the Dent de Vilard had been used by both parties without coming to extremities; it stood as a sort of party wall between the communes of Riceys and les Rouxey, yielding little profit. Indeed, the object in dispute, being covered with snow for six months in the year, was of a nature to cool their ardor. Thus it required all the hot blast by which the revolution of 1830 inflamed the advocates of the people, to stir up this matter, by which Monsieur Chantonnit, the

Maire of Riceys, hoped to give a dramatic turn to his career on the peaceful frontier of Switzerland, and to immortalize his term of office. Chantonnit, as his name shows, was a native of Neuchatel.

"My dear father," said Rosalie, as they got into the boat again, "I agree with Modinier. If you wish to secure the joint possession of the Dent de Vilard, you must act with decision, and get a legal opinion which will protect you against this enterprising Chantonnit. Why should you be afraid? Get the famous lawyer Savaron--engage him at once, lest Chantonnit should place the interests of the village in his hands. The man who won the case for the Chapter against the town can certainly win that of Watteville *versus* Riceys! Besides," she added, "les Rouxey will some day be mine--not for a long time yet, I trust.-- Well, then do not leave me with a lawsuit on my hands. I like this place, I shall often live here, and add to it as much as possible. On those banks," and she pointed to the feet of the two hills, "I shall cut flowerbeds and make the loveliest English gardens. Let us go to Besancon and bring back with us the Abbe de Grancey, Monsieur Savaron, and my mother, if she cares to come. You can then make up your mind; but in your place I should have done so already. Your name is Watteville, and you are afraid of a fight! If you should lose your case--well, I will never reproach you by a word!"

"Oh, if that is the way you take it," said the Baron, "I am quite ready; I will see the lawyer."

"Besides a lawsuit is really great fun. It brings some interest into life, with coming and going and raging over it. You will have a great deal to do before you can get hold of the judges.--We did not see the Abbe de Grancey for three weeks, he was so busy!"

"But the very existence of the Chapter was involved," said Monsieur de Watteville; "and then the Archbishop's pride, his conscience, everything that makes up the life of the priesthood, was at stake. That Savaron does not know what he did for the Chapter! He saved it!"

"Listen to me," said his daughter in his ear, "if you secure Monsieur de Savaron, you will gain your suit, won't you? Well, then, let me advise you. You cannot get at Monsieur Savaron excepting through Monsieur de Grancey. Take my word for it, and let us together talk to the dear Abbe without my mother's presence at the interview, for I know a way of persuading him to bring the lawyer to us."

"It will be very difficult to avoid mentioning it to your mother!"

"The Abbe de Grancey will settle that afterwards. But just make up your mind to promise your vote to Monsieur Savaron at the next election, and you will see!"

"Go to the election! take the oath?" cried the Baron de Watteville.

"What then!" said she.

"And what will your mother say?"

"She may even desire you to do it," replied Rosalie, knowing as she did from Albert's letter to Leopold how deeply the Vicar-General had pledged himself.

Four days after, the Abbe de Grancey called very early one morning on Albert de Savarus, having announced his visit the day before. The old priest had come to win over the great lawyer to the house of the Wattevilles, a proceeding which shows how much tact and subtlety Rosalie must have employed in an underhand way.

"What can I do for you, Monsieur le Vicaire-General?" asked Savarus.

The Abbe, who told his story with admirable frankness, was coldly heard by Albert.

"Monsieur l'Abbe," said he, "it is out of the question that I should defend the interests of the Wattevilles, and you shall understand why. My part in this town is to remain perfectly neutral. I will display no colors; I must remain a mystery till the eve of my election. Now, to plead for the Wattevilles would mean nothing in Paris, but here!-- Here, where everything is discussed, I should be supposed by every one to be an ally of your Faubourg Saint-Germain."

"What! do you suppose that you can remain unknown on the day of the election, when the candidates must oppose each other? It must then become known that your name is Savaron de Savarus, that you have held the appointment of Master of Appeals, that you are a man of the Restoration!"

"On the day of the election," said Savarus, "I will be all I am expected to be; and I intend to speak at the preliminary meetings."

"If you have the support of Monsieur de Watteville and his party, you will get a hundred votes in a mass, and far more to be trusted than those on which you rely. It is always possible to produce division of interests; convictions are inseparable."

"The deuce is in it!" said Savarus. "I am attached to you, and I could do a great deal for you, Father! Perhaps we may compound with the Devil. Whatever Monsieur de Watteville's business may be, by engaging Girardet, and prompting him, it will be possible to drag the proceedings out till the elections are over. I will not undertake to plead till the day after I am returned."

"Do this one thing," said the Abbe. "Come to the Hotel de Rupt: there is a young person of nineteen there who, one of these days, will have a hundred thousand francs a year, and you can seem to be paying your court to her--"

"Ah! the young lady I sometimes see in the kiosk?"

"Yes, Mademoiselle Rosalie," replied the Abbe de Grancey. "You are ambitious. If she takes a fancy to you, you may be everything an ambitious man can wish--who knows? A Minister perhaps. A man can always be a Minister who adds a hundred thousand francs a year to your amazing talents."

"Monsieur l'Abbe, if Mademoiselle de Watteville had three times her fortune, and adored me into the bargain, it would be impossible that I should marry her--"

"You are married?" exclaimed the Abbe.

"Not in church nor before the Maire, but morally speaking," said Savarus.

"That is even worse when a man cares about it as you seem to care," replied the Abbe. "Everything that is not done, can be undone. Do not stake your fortune and your prospects on a woman's liking, any more than a wise man counts on a dead man's shoes before starting on his way."

"Let us say no more about Mademoiselle de Watteville," said Albert gravely, "and agree as to the facts. At your desire--for I have a regard and respect for you--I will appear for Monsieur de Watteville, but after the elections. Until then Girardet must conduct the case under my instructions. That is the most I can do."

"But there are questions involved which can only be settled after inspection of the localities," said the Vicar-General.

"Girardet can go," said Savarus. "I cannot allow myself, in the face of a town I know so well, to take any step which might compromise the supreme interests that lie beyond my election."

The Abbe left Savarus after giving him a keen look, in which he seemed to be laughing at the young athlete's uncompromising politics, while admiring his firmness.

"Ah! I would have dragged my father into a lawsuit--I would have done anything to get him here!" cried Rosalie to herself, standing in the kiosk and looking at the lawyer in his room, the day after Albert's interview with the Abbe, who had reported the result to her father. "I would have committed any mortal sin, and you will not enter the Wattevilles' drawing-room; I may not hear your fine voice! You make conditions when your help is required by the Wattevilles and the Rupts!--Well, God knows, I meant to be content with these small joys; with seeing you, hearing you speak, going with you to les Rouxey, that your presence might to me make the place sacred. That was all I asked. But now--now I mean to be your wife.--Yes, yes; look at *her* portrait, at *her* drawing-room, *her* bedroom, at the four sides of *her* villa, the points of view from *her* gardens. You expect her statue? I will make her marble herself towards you!--After all, the woman does not love. Art, science, books, singing, music, have absorbed half her senses and her intelligence. She is old, too; she is past thirty; my Albert will not be happy!"

"What is the matter that you stay here, Rosalie?" asked her mother, interrupting her reflections. "Monsieur de Soulas is in the drawing-room, and he observed your attitude, which certainly betrays more thoughtfulness than is due at your age."

"Then, is Monsieur de Soulas a foe to thought?" asked Rosalie.

"Then you were thinking?" said Madame de Watteville.

"Why, yes, mamma."

"Why, no! you were not thinking. You were staring at that lawyer's window with an attention that is neither becoming, nor decent, and which Monsieur de Soulas, of all men, ought never to have observed."

"Why?" said Rosalie.

"It is time," said the Baroness, "that you should know what our intentions are. Amedee likes you, and you will not be unhappy as Comtesse de Soulas."

Rosalie, as white as a lily, made no reply, so completely was she stupefied by contending feelings. And yet in the presence of the man she had this instant begun to hate vehemently, she forced the kind of smile which a ballet-dancer puts on for the public. Nay, she could even laugh; she had the strength to conceal her rage, which presently subsided, for she was determined to make use of this fat simpleton to further her designs.

"Monsieur Amedee," said she, at the moment when her mother was walking ahead of them in the garden, affecting to leave the young people together, "were you not aware that Monsieur Albert Savaron de Savarus is a Legitimist?"

"A Legitimist?"

"Until 1830 he was Master of Appeals to the Council of State, attached
to the supreme Ministerial Council, and in favor with the Dauphin and
Dauphiness. It would be very good of you to say nothing against him,
but it would be better still if you would attend the election this
year, carry the day, and hinder that poor Monsieur de Chavoncourt from
representing the town of Besancon."

"What sudden interest have you in this Savaron?"

"Monsieur Albert Savaron de Savarus, the natural son of the Comte de
Savarus--pray keep the secret of my indiscretion--if he is returned
deputy, will be our advocate in the suit about les Rouxey. Les Rouxey,
my father tells me, will be my property; I intend to live there, it is
a lovely place! I should be broken-hearted at seeing that fine piece
of the great de Watteville's work destroyed."

"The devil!" thought Amedee, as he left the house. "The heiress is not
such a fool as her mother thinks her."

Monsieur de Chavoncourt is a Royalist, of the famous 221. Hence, from
the day after the revolution of July, he always preached the salutary
doctrine of taking the oaths and resisting the present order of
things, after the pattern of the Tories against the Whigs in England.
This doctrine was not acceptable to the Legitimists, who, in their
defeat, had the wit to divide in their opinions, and to trust to the
force of inertia and to Providence. Monsieur de Chavoncourt was not
wholly trusted by his own party, but seemed to the Moderates the best
man to choose; they preferred the triumph of his half-hearted opinions
to the acclamation of a Republican who should combine the votes of the
enthusiasts and the patriots. Monsieur de Chavoncourt, highly
respected in Besancon, was the representative of an old parliamentary
family; his fortune, of about fifteen thousand francs a year, was not
an offence to anybody, especially as he had a son and three daughters.

With such a family, fifteen thousand francs a year are a mere nothing. Now when, under these circumstances, the father of the family is above bribery, it would be hard if the electors did not esteem him. Electors wax enthusiastic over a ***beau ideal*** of parliamentary virtue, just as the audience in the pit do at the representation of the generous sentiments they so little practise.

Madame de Chavoncourt, at this time a woman of forty, was one of the beauties of Besancon. While the Chamber was sitting, she lived meagrely in one of their country places to recoup herself by economy for Monsieur de Chavoncourt's expenses in Paris. In the winter she received very creditably once a week, on Tuesdays, understanding her business as mistress of the house. Young Chavoncourt, a youth of two-and-twenty, and another young gentleman, named Monsieur de Vauchelles, no richer than Amedee and his school-friend, were his intimate allies. They made excursions together to Granvelle, and sometimes went out shooting; they were so well known to be inseparable that they were invited to the country together.

Rosalie, who was intimate with the Chavoncourt girls, knew that the three young men had no secrets from each other. She reflected that if Monsieur de Soulas should repeat her words, it would be to his two companions. Now, Monsieur de Vauchelles had his matrimonial plans, as Amedee had his; he wished to marry Victoire, the eldest of the Chavoncourts, on whom an old aunt was to settle an estate worth seven thousand francs a year, and a hundred thousand francs in hard cash, when the contract was to be signed. Victoire was this aunt's god-daughter and favorite niece. Consequently, young Chavoncourt and his friend Vauchelles would be sure to warn Monsieur de Chavoncourt of the danger he was in from Albert's candidature.

But this did not satisfy Rosalie. She sent the Prefet of the department a letter written with her left hand, signed "A friend to

Louis Philippe," in which she informed him of the secret intentions of Monsieur Albert de Savarus, pointing out the serious support a Royalist orator might give to Berryer, and revealing to him the deeply artful course pursued by the lawyer during his two years' residence at Besancon. The Prefet was a capable man, a personal enemy of the Royalist party, devoted by conviction to the Government of July--in short, one of those men of whom, in the Rue de Grenelle, the Minister of the Interior could say, "We have a capital Prefet at Besancon."-- The Prefet read the letter, and, in obedience to its instructions, he burnt it.

Rosalie aimed at preventing Albert's election, so as to keep him five years longer at Besancon.

At that time an election was a fight between parties, and in order to win, the Ministry chose its ground by choosing the moment when it would give battle. The elections were therefore not to take place for three months yet. When a man's whole life depends on an election, the period that elapses between the issuing of the writs for convening the electoral bodies, and the day fixed for their meetings, is an interval during which ordinary vitality is suspended. Rosalie fully understood how much latitude Albert's absorbed state would leave her during these three months. By promising Mariette--as she afterwards confessed--to take both her and Jerome into her service, she induced the maid to bring her all the letters Albert might sent to Italy, and those addressed to him from that country. And all the time she was pondering these machinations, the extraordinary girl was working slippers for her father with the most innocent air in the world. She even made a greater display than ever of candor and simplicity, quite understanding how valuable that candor and innocence would be to her ends.

"My daughter grows quite charming!" said Madame de Watteville.

Two months before the election a meeting was held at the house of
Monsieur Boucher senior, composed of the contractor who expected to
get the work for the aqueduct for the Arcier waters; of Monsieur
Boucher's father-in-law; of Monsieur Granet, the influential man to
whom Savarus had done a service, and who was to nominate him as a
candidate; of Girardet the lawyer; of the printer of the Eastern
Review; and of the President of the Chamber of Commerce. In fact, the
assembly consisted of twenty-seven persons in all, men who in the
provinces are regarded as bigwigs. Each man represented on an average
six votes, but in estimating their values they said ten, for men
always begin by exaggerating their own influence. Among these twenty-
seven was one who was wholly devoted to the Prefet, one false brother
who secretly looked for some favor from the Ministry, either for
himself or for some one belonging to him.

At this preliminary meeting, it was agreed that Savaron the lawyer
should be named as candidate, a motion received with such enthusiasm
as no one looked for from Besancon. Albert, waiting at home for Alfred
Boucher to fetch him, was chatting with the Abbe de Grancey, who was
interested in this absorbing ambition. Albert had appreciated the
priest's vast political capacities; and the priest, touched by the
young man's entreaties, had been willing to become his guide and
adviser in this culminating struggle. The Chapter did not love
Monsieur de Chavoncourt, for it was his wife's brother-in-law, as
President of the Tribunal, who had lost the famous suit for them in
the lower Court.

"You are betrayed, my dear fellow," said the shrewd and worthy Abbe,
in that gentle, calm voice which old priests acquire.

"Betrayed!" cried the lover, struck to the heart.

"By whom I know not at all," the priest replied. "But at the
Prefecture your plans are known, and your hand read like a book. At
this moment I have no advice to give you. Such affairs need
consideration. As for this evening, take the bull by the horns,
anticipate the blow. Tell them all your previous life, and thus you
will mitigate the effect of the discovery on the good folks of
Besancon."

"Oh, I was prepared for it," said Albert in a broken voice.

"You would not benefit by my advice; you had the opportunity of making
an impression at the Hotel de Rupt; you do not know the advantage you
would have gained--"

"What?"

"The unanimous support of the Royalists, an immediate readiness to go
to the election--in short, above a hundred votes. Adding to these
what, among ourselves, we call the ecclesiastical vote, though you
were not yet nominated, you were master of the votes by ballot. Under
such circumstances, a man may temporize, may make his way--"

Alfred Boucher when he came in, full of enthusiasm, to announce the
decision of the preliminary meeting, found the Vicar-General and the
lawyer cold, calm, and grave.

"Good-night, Monsieur l'Abbe," said Albert. "We will talk of your
business at greater length when the elections are over."

And he took Alfred's arm, after pressing Monsieur de Grancey's hand
with meaning. The priest looked at the ambitious man, whose face at
that moment wore the lofty expression which a general may have when he
hears the first gun fired for a battle. He raised his eyes to heaven,

and left the room, saying to himself, "What a priest he would make!"

Eloquence is not at the Bar. The pleader rarely puts forth the real powers of his soul; if he did, he would die of it in a few years. Eloquence is, nowadays, rarely in the pulpit; but it is found on certain occasions in the Chamber of Deputies, when an ambitious man stakes all to win all, or, stung by a myriad darts, at a given moment bursts into speech. But it is still more certainly found in some privileged beings, at the inevitable hour when their claims must either triumph or be wrecked, and when they are forced to speak. Thus at this meeting, Albert Savarus, feeling the necessity of winning himself some supporters, displayed all the faculties of his soul and the resources of his intellect. He entered the room well, without awkwardness or arrogance, without weakness, without cowardice, quite gravely, and was not dismayed at finding himself among twenty or thirty men. The news of the meeting and of its determination had already brought a few docile sheep to follow the bell.

Before listening to Monsieur Boucher, who was about to deluge him with a speech announcing the decision of the Boucher Committee, Albert begged for silence, and, as he shook hands with Monsieur Boucher, tried to warn him, by a sign, of an unexpected danger.

"My young friend, Alfred Boucher, has just announced to me the honor you have done me. But before that decision is irrevocable," said the lawyer, "I think that I ought to explain to you who and what your candidate is, so as to leave you free to take back your word if my declaration should disturb your conscience!"

This exordium was followed by profound silence. Some of the men thought it showed a noble impulse.

Albert gave a sketch of his previous career, telling them his real

name, his action under the Restoration, and revealing himself as a new
man since his arrival at Besancon, while pledging himself for the
future. This address held his hearers breathless, it was said. These
men, all with different interests, were spellbound by the brilliant
eloquence that flowed at boiling heat from the heart and soul of this
ambitious spirit. Admiration silenced reflection. Only one thing was
clear--the thing which Albert wished to get into their heads:

Was it not far better for the town to have one of those men who are
born to govern society at large than a mere voting-machine? A
statesman carries power with him. A commonplace deputy, however
incorruptible, is but a conscience. What a glory for Provence to have
found a Mirabeau, to return the only statesman since 1830 that the
revolution of July had produced!

Under the pressure of this eloquence, all the audience believed it
great enough to become a splendid political instrument in the hands of
their representative. They all saw in Albert Savaron, Savarus the
great Minister. And, reading the secret calculations of his
constituents, the clever candidate gave them to understand that they
would be the first to enjoy the right of profiting by his influence.

This confession of faith, this ambitious programme, this retrospect of
his life and character was, according to the only man present who was
capable of judging of Savarus (he has since become one of the leading
men of Besancon), a masterpiece of skill and of feeling, of fervor,
interest, and fascination. This whirlwind carried away the electors.
Never had any man had such a triumph. But, unfortunately, speech, a
weapon only for close warfare, has only an immediate effect.
Reflection kills the word when the word ceases to overpower
reflection. If the votes had then been taken, Albert's name would
undoubtedly have come out of the ballot-box. At the moment, he was
conqueror. But he must conquer every day for two months.

Albert went home quivering. The townsfolk had applauded him, and he had achieved the great point of silencing beforehand the malignant talk to which his early career might give rise. The commercial interest of Besancon had nominated the lawyer, Albert Savaron de Savarus, as its candidate.

Alfred Boucher's enthusiasm, at first infectious, presently became blundering.

The Prefet, alarmed by this success, set to work to count the Ministerial votes, and contrived to have a secret interview with Monsieur de Chavoncourt, so as to effect a coalition in their common interests. Every day, without Albert's being able to discover how, the voters in the Boucher committee diminished in number.

Nothing could resist the slow grinding of the Prefecture. Three of four clever men would say to Albert's clients, "Will the deputy defend you and win your lawsuits? Will he give you advice, draw up your contracts, arrange your compromises?--He will be your slave for five years longer, if, instead of returning him to the Chamber, you only hold out the hope of his going there five years hence."

This calculation did Savarus all the more mischief, because the wives of some of the merchants had already made it. The parties interested in the matter of the bridge and that of the water from Arcier could not hold out against a talking-to from a clever Ministerialist, who proved to them that their safety lay at the Prefecture, and not in the hands of an ambitious man. Each day was a check for Savarus, though each day the battle was led by him and fought by his lieutenants--a battle of words, speeches, and proceedings. He dared not go to the Vicar-General, and the Vicar-General never showed himself. Albert rose and went to bed in a fever, his brain on fire.

At last the day dawned of the first struggle, practically the show of hands; the votes are counted, the candidates estimate their chances, and clever men can prophesy their failure or success. It is a decent hustings, without the mob, but formidable; agitation, though it is not allowed any physical display, as it is in England, is not the less profound. The English fight these battles with their fists, the French with hard words. Our neighbors have a scrimmage, the French try their fate by cold combinations calmly worked out. This particular political business is carried out in opposition to the character of the two nations.

The Radical party named their candidate; Monsieur de Chavoncourt came forward; then Albert appeared, and was accused by the Chavoncourt committee and the Radicals of being an uncompromising man of the Right, a second Berryer. The Ministry had their candidate, a stalking-horse, useful only to receive the purely Ministerial votes. The votes, thus divided, gave no result. The Republican candidate had twenty, the Ministry got fifty, Albert had seventy, Monsieur de Chavoncourt obtained sixty-seven. But the Prefet's party had perfidiously made thirty of its most devoted adherents vote for Albert, so as to deceive the enemy. The votes for Monsieur de Chavoncourt, added to the eighty votes--the real number--at the disposal of the Prefecture, would carry the election, if only the Prefet could succeed in gaining over a few of the Radicals. A hundred and sixty votes were not recorded: those of Monsieur de Grancey's following and the Legitimists.

The show of hands at an election, like a dress rehearsal at a theatre, is the most deceptive thing in the world. Albert Savarus came home, putting a brave face on the matter, but half dead. He had had the wit, the genius, or the good luck to gain, within the last fortnight, two staunch supporters--Girardet's father-in-law and a very shrewd old merchant to whom Monsieur de Grancey had sent him. These two worthy men, his self-appointed spies, affected to be Albert's most ardent opponents in the hostile camp. Towards the end of the show of hands they informed Savarus, through the medium of Monsieur Boucher, that thirty voters, unknown, were working against him in his party, playing the same trick that they were playing for his benefit on the other side.

A criminal marching to execution could not suffer as Albert suffered as he went home from the hall where his fate was at stake. The despairing lover could endure no companionship. He walked through the streets alone, between eleven o'clock and midnight. At one in the morning, Albert, to whom sleep had been unknown for the past three days, was sitting in his library in a deep armchair, his face as pale as if he were dying, his hands hanging limp, in a forlorn attitude worthy of the Magdalen. Tears hung on his long lashes, tears that dim the eyes, but do not fall; fierce thought drinks them up, the fire of the soul consumes them. Alone, he might weep. And then, under the kiosk, he saw a white figure, which reminded him of Francesca.

"And for three months I have had no letter from her! What has become of her? I have not written for two months, but I warned her. Is she ill? Oh, my love! My life! Will you ever know what I have gone through? What a wretched constitution is mine! Have I an aneurism?" he asked himself, feeling his heart beat so violently that its pulses seemed audible in the silence like little grains of sand dropping on a big drum.

At this moment three distinct taps sounded on his door; Albert hastened to open it, and almost fainted with joy at seeing the Vicar-General's cheerful and triumphant mien. Without a word, he threw his arms round the Abbe de Grancey, held him fast, and clasped him closely, letting his head fall on the old man's shoulder. He was a child again; he cried as he had cried on hearing that Francesca

Soderini was a married woman. He betrayed his weakness to no one but to this priest, on whose face shone the light of hope. The priest had been sublime, and as shrewd as he was sublime.

"Forgive me, dear Abbe, but you come at one of those moments when the man vanishes, for you are not to think me vulgarly ambitious."

"Oh! I know," replied the Abbe. "You wrote 'Ambition for love's sake!'--Ah! my son, it was love in despair that made me a priest in 1786, at the age of two-and-twenty. In 1788 I was in charge of a parish. I know life.--I have refused three bishoprics already; I mean to die at Besancon."

"Come and see her!" cried Savarus, seizing a candle, and leading the Abbe into the handsome room where hung the portrait of the Duchesse d'Argaiolo, which he lighted up.

"She is one of those women who are born to reign!" said the Vicar-General, understanding how great an affection Albert showed him by this mark of confidence. "But there is pride on that brow; it is implacable; she would never forgive an insult! It is the Archangel Michael, the angel of Execution, the inexorable angel--'All or nothing' is the motto of this type of angel. There is something divinely pitiless in that head."

"You have guessed well," cried Savarus. "But, my dear Abbe, for more than twelve years now she had reigned over my life, and I have not a thought for which to blame myself--"

"Ah! if you could only say the same of God!" said the priest with simplicity. "Now, to talk of your affairs. For ten days I have been at work for you. If you are a real politician, this time you will follow my advice. You would not be where you are now if you would have gone

to the Wattevilles when I first told you. But you must go there
to-morrow; I will take you in the evening. The Rouxey estates are in
danger; the case must be defended within three days. The election will
not be over in three days. They will take good care not to appoint
examiners the first day. There will be several voting days, and you
will be elected by ballot--"

"How can that be?" asked Savarus.

"By winning the Rouxey lawsuit you will gain eighty Legitimist votes;
add them to the thirty I can command, and you have a hundred and ten.
Then, as twenty remain to you of the Boucher committee, you will have
a hundred and thirty in all."

"Well," said Albert, "we must get seventy-five more."

"Yes," said the priest, "since all the rest are Ministerial. But, my
son, you have two hundred votes, and the Prefecture no more than a
hundred and eighty."

"I have two hundred votes?" said Albert, standing stupid with
amazement, after starting to his feet as if shot up by a spring.

"You have those of Monsieur de Chavoncourt," said the Abbe.

"How?" said Albert.

"You will marry Mademoiselle Sidonie de Chavoncourt."

"Never!"

"You will marry Mademoiselle Sidonie de Chavoncourt," the priest
repeated coldly.

"But you see--she is inexorable," said Albert, pointing to Francesca.

"You will marry Mademoiselle Sidonie de Chavoncourt," said the Abbe calmly for the third time.

This time Albert understood. The Vicar-General would not be implicated in a scheme which at last smiled on the despairing politician. A word more would have compromised the priest's dignity and honor.

"To-morrow evening at the Hotel de Rupt you will meet Madame de Chavoncourt and her second daughter. You can thank her beforehand for what she is going to do for you, and tell her that your gratitude is unbounded, that you are hers body and soul, that henceforth your future is that of her family. You are quite disinterested, for you have so much confidence in yourself that you regard the nomination as deputy as a sufficient fortune.

"You will have a struggle with Madame de Chavoncourt; she will want you to pledge your word. All your future life, my son, lies in that evening. But, understand clearly, I have nothing to do with it. I am answerable only for Legitimist voters; I have secured Madame de Watteville, and that means all the aristocracy of Besancon. Amedee de Soulas and Vauchelles, who will both vote for you, have won over the young men; Madame de Watteville will get the old ones. As to my electors, they are infallible."

"And who on earth has gained over Madame de Chavoncourt?" asked Savarus.

"Ask me no questions," replied the Abbe. "Monsieur de Chavoncourt, who has three daughters to marry, is not capable of increasing his wealth. Though Vauchelles marries the eldest without anything from her father,

because her old aunt is to settle something on her, what is to become
of the two others? Sidonie is sixteen, and your ambition is as good as
a gold mine. Some one has told Madame de Chavoncourt that she will do
better by getting her daughter married than by sending her husband to
waste his money in Paris. That some one manages Madame de Chavoncourt,
and Madame de Chavoncourt manages her husband."

"That is enough, my dear Abbe. I understand. When once I am returned
as deputy, I have somebody's fortune to make, and by making it large
enough I shall be released from my promise. In me you have a son, a
man who will owe his happiness to you. Great heavens! what have I done
to deserve so true a friend?"

"You won a triumph for the Chapter," said the Vicar-General, smiling.
"Now, as to all this, be as secret as the tomb. We are nothing, we
have done nothing. If we were known to have meddled in election
matters, we should be eaten up alive by the Puritans of the Left--who
do worse--and blamed by some of our own party, who want everything.
Madame de Chavoncourt has no suspicion of my share in all this. I have
confided in no one but Madame de Watteville, whom we may trust as we
trust ourselves."

"I will bring the Duchess to you to be blessed!" cried Savarus.

After seeing out the old priest, Albert went to bed in the swaddling
clothes of power.

Next evening, as may well be supposed, by nine o'clock Madame la
Baronne de Watteville's rooms were crowded by the aristocracy of
Besancon in convocation extraordinary. They were discussing the
exceptional step of going to the poll, to oblige the daughter of the

Rupts. It was known that the former Master of Appeals, the secretary of one of the most faithful ministers under the Elder Branch, was to be presented that evening. Madame de Chavoncourt was there with her second daughter Sidonie, exquisitely dressed, while her elder sister, secure of her lover, had not indulged in any of the arts of the toilet. In country towns these little things are remarked. The Abbe de Grancey's fine and clever head was to be seen moving from group to group, listening to everything, seeming to be apart from it all, but uttering those incisive phrases which sum up a question and direct the issue.

"If the Elder Branch were to return," said he to an old statesman of seventy, "what politicians would they find?"--"Berryer, alone on his bench, does not know which way to turn; if he had sixty votes, he would often scotch the wheels of the Government and upset Ministries!" --"The Duc de Fitz-James is to be nominated at Toulouse."--"You will enable Monsieur de Watteville to win his lawsuit."--"If you vote for Monsieur Savarus, the Republicans will vote with you rather than with the Moderates!" etc., etc.

At nine o'clock Albert had not arrived. Madame de Watteville was disposed to regard such delay as an impertinence.

"My dear Baroness," said Madame de Chavoncourt, "do not let such serious issues turn on such a trifle. The varnish on his boots is not dry--or a consultation, perhaps, detains Monsieur de Savarus."

Rosalie shot a side glance at Madame de Chavoncourt.

"She is very lenient to Monsieur de Savarus," she whispered to her mother.

"You see," said the Baroness with a smile, "there is a question of a marriage between Sidonie and Monsieur de Savarus."

Mademoiselle de Watteville hastily went to a window looking out over the garden.

At ten o'clock Albert de Savarus had not yet appeared. The storm that threatened now burst. Some of the gentlemen sat down to cards, finding the thing intolerable. The Abbe de Grancey, who did not know what to think, went to the window where Rosalie was hidden, and exclaimed aloud in his amazement, "He must be dead!"

The Vicar-General stepped out into the garden, followed by Monsieur de Watteville and his daughter, and they all three went up to the kiosk. In Albert's rooms all was dark; not a light was to be seen.

"Jerome!" cried Rosalie, seeing the servant in the yard below. The Abbe looked at her with astonishment. "Where in the world is your master?" she asked the man, who came to the foot of the wall.

"Gone--in a post-chaise, mademoiselle."

"He is ruined!" exclaimed the Abbe de Grancey, "or he is happy!"

The joy of triumph was not so effectually concealed on Rosalie's face that the Vicar-General could not detect it. He affected to see nothing.

"What can this girl have had to do with this business?" he asked himself.

They all three returned to the drawing-room, where Monsieur de Watteville announced the strange, the extraordinary, the prodigious news of the lawyer's departure, without any reason assigned for his evasion. By half-past eleven only fifteen persons remained, among them Madame de Chavoncourt and the Abbe de Godenars, another Vicar-General, a man of about forty, who hoped for a bishopric, the two Chavoncourt girls, and Monsieur de Vauchelles, the Abbe de Grancey, Rosalie, Amedee de Soulas, and a retired magistrate, one of the most influential members of the upper circle of Besancon, who had been very eager for Albert's election. The Abbe de Grancey sat down by the Baroness in such a position as to watch Rosalie, whose face, usually pale, wore a feverish flush.

"What can have happened to Monsieur de Savarus?" said Madame de Chavoncourt.

At this moment a servant in livery brought in a letter for the Abbe de Grancey on a silver tray.

"Pray read it," said the Baroness.

The Vicar-General read the letter; he saw Rosalie suddenly turn as white as her kerchief.

"She recognizes the writing," said he to himself, after glancing at the girl over his spectacles. He folded up the letter, and calmly put it in his pocket without a word. In three minutes he had met three looks from Rosalie which were enough to make him guess everything.

"She is in love with Albert Savarus!" thought the Vicar-General.

He rose and took leave. He was going towards the door when, in the next room, he was overtaken by Rosalie, who said:

"Monsieur de Grancey, it was from Albert!"

"How do you know that it was his writing, to recognize it from so far?"

The girl's reply, caught as she was in the toils of her impatience and rage, seemed to the Abbe sublime.

"I love him!--What is the matter?" she said after a pause.

"He gives up the election."

Rosalie put her finger to her lip.

"I ask you to be as secret as if it were a confession," said she before returning to the drawing-room. "If there is an end of the election, there is an end of the marriage with Sidonie."

In the morning, on her way to Mass, Mademoiselle de Watteville heard from Mariette some of the circumstances which had prompted Albert's disappearance at the most critical moment of his life.

"Mademoiselle, an old gentleman from Paris arrived yesterday morning at the Hotel National; he came in his own carriage with four horses, and a courier in front, and a servant. Indeed, Jerome, who saw the carriage returning, declares he could only be a prince or a *milord*."

"Was there a coronet on the carriage?" asked Rosalie.

"I do not know," said Mariette. "Just as two was striking he came to call on Monsieur Savarus, and sent in his card; and when he saw it, Jerome says Monsieur turned as pale as a sheet, and said he was to be shown in. As he himself locked the door, it is impossible to tell what the old gentleman and the lawyer said to each other; but they were together above an hour, and then the old gentleman, with the lawyer, called up his servant. Jerome saw the servant go out again with an immense package, four feet long, which looked like a great painting on canvas. The old gentleman had in his hand a large parcel of papers. Monsieur Savaron was paler than death, and he, so proud, so dignified, was in a state to be pitied. But he treated the old gentleman so respectfully that he could not have been politer to the King himself. Jerome and Monsieur Albert Savaron escorted the gentleman to his carriage, which was standing with the horses in. The courier started on the stroke of three.

"Monsieur Savaron went straight to the Prefecture, and from that to Monsieur Gentillet, who sold him the old traveling carriage that used to belong to Madame de Saint-Vier before she died; then he ordered post horses for six o'clock. He went home to pack; no doubt he wrote a lot of letters; finally, he settled everything with Monsieur Girardet, who went to him and stayed till seven. Jerome carried a note to Monsieur Boucher, with whom his master was to have dined; and then, at half-past seven, the lawyer set out, leaving Jerome with three months' wages, and telling him to find another place.

"He left his keys with Monsieur Girardet, whom he took home, and at his house, Jerome says, he took a plate of soup, for at half-past seven Monsieur Girardet had not yet dined. When Monsieur Savaron got into the carriage he looked like death. Jerome, who, of course, saw his master off, heard him tell the postilion 'The Geneva Road!' "

"Did Jerome ask the name of the stranger at the Hotel National?"

"As the old gentleman did not mean to stay, he was not asked for it. The servant, by his orders no doubt, pretended not to speak French."

"And the letter which came so late to Abbe de Grancey?" said Rosalie.

"It was Monsieur Girardet, no doubt, who ought to have delivered it; but Jerome says that poor Monsieur Girardet, who was much attached to lawyer Savaron, was as much upset as he was. So he who came so mysteriously, as Mademoiselle Galard says, is gone away just as mysteriously."

After hearing this narrative, Mademoiselle de Watteville fell into a brooding and absent mood, which everybody could see. It is useless to say anything of the commotion that arose in Besancon on the disappearance of Monsieur Savaron. It was understood that the Prefect had obliged him with the greatest readiness by giving him at once a passport across the frontier, for he was thus quit of his only opponent. Next day Monsieur de Chavoncourt was carried to the top by a majority of a hundred and forty votes.

"Jack is gone by the way he came," said an elector on hearing of Albert Savaron's flight.

This event lent weight to the prevailing prejudice at Besancon against strangers; indeed, two years previously they had received confirmation from the affair of the Republican newspaper. Ten days later Albert de Savarus was never spoken of again. Only three persons--Girardet the attorney, the Vicar-General, and Rosalie--were seriously affected by his disappearance. Girardet knew that the white-haired stranger was Prince Soderini, for he had seen his card, and he told the Vicar-General; but Rosalie, better informed than either of them, had known for three months past that the Duc d'Argaiolo was dead.

In the month of April 1836 no one had had any news from or of Albert de Savarus. Jerome and Mariette were to be married, but the Baroness confidentially desired her maid to wait till her daughter was married, saying that the two weddings might take place at the same time.

"It is time that Rosalie should be married," said the Baroness one day to Monsieur de Watteville. "She is nineteen, and she is fearfully altered in these last months."

"I do not know what ails her," said the Baron.

"When fathers do not know what ails their daughters, mothers can guess," said the Baroness; "we must get her married."

"I am quite willing," said the Baron. "I shall give her les Rouxey now that the Court has settled our quarrel with the authorities of Riceys by fixing the boundary line at three hundred feet up the side of the Dent de Vilard. I am having a trench made to collect all the water and carry it into the lake. The village did not appeal, so the decision is final."

"It has never occurred to you," said Madame de Watteville, "that this decision cost me thirty thousand francs handed over to Chantonnit. That peasant would take nothing else; he sold us peace.--If you give away les Rouxey, you will have nothing left," said the Baroness.

"I do not need much," said the Baron; "I am breaking up."

"You eat like an ogre!"

"Just so. But however much I may eat, I feel my legs get weaker and weaker--"

"It is from working the lathe," said his wife.

"I do not know," said he.

"We will marry Rosalie to Monsieur de Soulas; if you give her les Rouxey, keep the life interest. I will give them fifteen thousand francs a year in the funds. Our children can live here; I do not see that they are much to be pitied."

"No. I shall give them les Rouxey out and out. Rosalie is fond of les Rouxey."

"You are a queer man with your daughter! It does not occur to you to ask me if I am fond of les Rouxey."

Rosalie, at once sent for, was informed that she was to marry Monsieur de Soulas one day early in the month of May.

"I am very much obliged to you, mother, and to you too, father, for having thought of settling me; but I do not mean to marry; I am very happy with you."

"Mere speeches!" said the Baroness. "You are not in love with Monsieur de Soulas, that is all."

"If you insist on the plain truth, I will never marry Monsieur de Soulas--"

"Oh! the *never* of a girl of nineteen!" retorted her mother, with a bitter smile.

"The *never* of Mademoiselle de Watteville," said Rosalie with firm decision. "My father, I imagine, has no intention of making me marry against my wishes?"

"No, indeed no!" said the poor Baron, looking affectionately at his daughter.

"Very well!" said the Baroness, sternly controlling the rage of a bigot startled at finding herself unexpectedly defied, "you yourself, Monsieur de Watteville, may take the responsibility of settling your daughter. Consider well, mademoiselle, for if you do not marry to my mind you will get nothing out of me!"

The quarrel thus begun between Madame de Watteville and her husband, who took his daughter's part, went so far that Rosalie and her father were obliged to spend the summer at les Rouxey; life at the Hotel de Rupt was unendurable. It thus became known in Besancon that Mademoiselle de Watteville had positively refused the Comte de Soulas.

After their marriage Mariette and Jerome came to les Rouxey to succeed to Modinier in due time. The Baron restored and repaired the house to suit his daughter's taste. When she heard that these improvements had cost about sixty thousand francs, and that Rosalie and her father were building a conservatory, the Baroness understood that there was a leaven of spite in her daughter. The Baron purchased various outlying plots, and a little estate worth thirty thousand francs. Madame de Watteville was told that, away from her, Rosalie showed masterly qualities, that she was taking steps to improve the value of les Rouxey, that she had treated herself to a riding habit and rode about; her father, whom she made very happy, who no longer complained of his health, and who was growing fat, accompanied her in her expeditions. As the Baroness' name-day grew near--her name was Louise--the Vicar-General came one day to les Rouxey, deputed, no doubt, by Madame de Watteville and Monsieur de Soulas, to negotiate a peace between mother and daughter.

"That little Rosalie has a head on her shoulders," said the folk of Besancon.

After handsomely paying up the ninety thousand francs spent on les Rouxey, the Baroness allowed her husband a thousand francs a month to live on; she would not put herself in the wrong. The father and daughter were perfectly willing to return to Besancon for the 15th of August, and to remain there till the end of the month.

When, after dinner, the Vicar-General took Mademoiselle de Watteville apart, to open the question of the marriage, by explaining to her that it was vain to think any more of Albert, of whom they had had no news for a year past, he was stopped at once by a sign from Rosalie. The strange girl took Monsieur de Grancey by the arm, and led him to a seat under a clump of rhododendrons, whence there was a view of the lake.

"Listen, dear Abbe," said she. "You whom I love as much as my father, for you had an affection for my Albert, I must at last confess that I committed crimes to become his wife, and he must be my husband.--Here; read this."

She held out to him a number of the *Gazette* which she had in her apron pocket, pointing out the following paragraph under the date of Florence, May 25th:--

"The wedding of Monsieur le Duc de Rhetore, eldest son of the Duc de Chaulieu, the former Ambassador, to Madame la Duchesse d'Argaiolo, *nee* Princess Soderini, was solemnized with great splendor. Numerous entertainments given in honor of the marriage are making Florence gay. The Duchess' fortune is one of the finest in Italy, for the late Duke left her everything.

"The woman he loved is married," said she. "I divided them."

"You? How?" asked the Abbe.

Rosalie was about to reply, when she was interrupted by a loud cry from two of the gardeners, following on the sound of a body falling into the water; she started, and ran off screaming, "Oh! father!"--The Baron had disappeared.

In trying to reach a piece of granite on which he fancied he saw the impression of a shell, a circumstance which would have contradicted some system of geology, Monsieur de Watteville had gone down the slope, lost his balance, and slipped into the lake, which, of course, was deepest close under the roadway. The men had the greatest difficulty in enabling the Baron to catch hold of a pole pushed down at the place where the water was bubbling, but at last they pulled him out, covered with mud, in which he had sunk; he was getting deeper and deeper in, by dint of struggling. Monsieur de Watteville had dined heavily, digestion was in progress, and was thus checked.

When he had been undressed, washed, and put to bed, he was in such evident danger that two servants at once set out on horseback: one to ride to Besancon, and the other to fetch the nearest doctor and surgeon. When Madame de Watteville arrived, eight hours later, with the first medical aid from Besancon, they found Monsieur de Watteville past all hope, in spite of the intelligent treatment of the Rouxey doctor. The fright had produced serious effusion on the brain, and the shock to the digestion was helping to kill the poor man.

This death, which would never have happened, said Madame de Watteville, if her husband had stayed at Besancon, was ascribed by her to her daughter's obstinacy. She took an aversion for Rosalie, abandoning herself to grief and regrets that were evidently exaggerated. She spoke of the Baron as "her dear lamb!"

The last of the Wattevilles was buried on an island in the lake at les Rouxey, where the Baroness had a little Gothic monument erected of white marble, like that called the tomb of Heloise at Pere-Lachaise.

A month after this catastrophe the mother and daughter had settled in the Hotel de Rupt, where they lived in savage silence. Rosalie was suffering from real sorrow, which had no visible outlet; she accused herself of her father's death, and she feared another disaster, much greater in her eyes, and very certainly her own work; neither Girardet the attorney nor the Abbe de Grancey could obtain any information concerning Albert. This silence was appalling. In a paroxysm of repentance she felt that she must confess to the Vicar-General the horrible machinations by which she had separated Francesca and Albert. They had been simple, but formidable. Mademoiselle de Watteville had intercepted Albert's letters to the Duchess as well as that in which Francesca announced her husband's illness, warning her lover that she could write to him no more during the time while she was devoted, as was her duty, to the care of the dying man. Thus, while Albert was wholly occupied with election matters, the Duchess had written him only two letters; one in which she told him that the Duc d'Argaiolo was in danger, and one announcing her widowhood--two noble and beautiful letters which Rosalie kept back.

After several nights' labor she succeeded in imitating Albert's writing very perfectly. She had substituted three letters of her own writing for three of Albert's, and the rough copies which she showed to the old priest made him shudder--the genius of evil was revealed in them to such perfection. Rosalie, writing in Albert's name, had prepared the Duchess for a change in the Frenchman's feelings, falsely representing him as faithless, and she had answered the news of the Duc d'Argaiolo's death by announcing the marriage ere long of Albert and Mademoiselle de Watteville. The two letters, intended to cross on the road, had, in fact, done so. The infernal cleverness with which the letters were written so much astonished the Vicar-General that he read them a second time. Francesca, stabbed to the heart by a girl who wanted to kill love in her rival, had answered the last in these four words: "You are free. Farewell."

"Purely moral crimes, which give no hold to human justice, are the most atrocious and detestable," said the Abbe severely. "God often punishes them on earth; herein lies the reason of the terrible catastrophes which to us seem inexplicable. Of all secret crimes buried in the mystery of private life, the most disgraceful is that of breaking the seal of a letter, or of reading it surreptitiously. Every one, whoever it may be, and urged by whatever reason, who is guilty of such an act has stained his honor beyond retrieving.

"Do you not feel all that is touching, that is heavenly in the story of the youthful page, falsely accused, and carrying the letter containing the order for his execution, who sets out without a thought of ill, and whom Providence protects and saves--miraculously, we say! But do you know wherein the miracle lies? Virtue has a glory as potent as that of innocent childhood.

"I say these things not meaning to admonish you," said the old priest, with deep grief. "I, alas! am not your spiritual director; you are not kneeling at the feet of God; I am your friend, appalled by dread of what your punishment may be. What has become of that unhappy Albert? Has he, perhaps, killed himself? There was tremendous passion under his assumption of calm. I understand now that old Prince Soderini, the father of the Duchess d'Argaiolo, came here to take back his daughter's letters and portraits. This was the thunderbolt that fell on Albert's head, and he went off, no doubt, to try to justify himself. But how is it that in fourteen months he has given us no news of himself?"

"Oh! if I marry him, he will be so happy!"

"Happy?--He does not love you. Besides, you have no great fortune to give him. Your mother detests you; you made her a fierce reply which rankles, and which will be your ruin. When she told you yesterday that obedience was the only way to repair your errors, and reminded you of the need for marrying, mentioning Amedee--'If you are so fond of him, marry him yourself, mother!'--Did you, or did you not, fling these words in her teeth?"

"Yes," said Rosalie.

"Well, I know her," Monsieur de Grancey went on. "In a few months she will be Comtesse de Soulas! She will be sure to have children; she will give Monsieur de Soulas forty thousand francs a year; she will benefit him in other ways, and reduce your share of her fortune as much as possible. You will be poor as long as she lives, and she is but eight-and-thirty! Your whole estate will be the land of les Rouxey, and the small share left to you after your father's legal debts are settled, if, indeed, your mother should consent to forego her claims on les Rouxey. From the point of view of material advantages, you have done badly for yourself; from the point of view of feeling, I imagine you have wrecked your life. Instead of going to your mother--" Rosalie shook her head fiercely.

"To your mother," the priest went on, "and to religion, where you would, at the first impulse of your heart, have found enlightenment, counsel, and guidance, you chose to act in your own way, knowing nothing of life, and listening only to passion!"

These words of wisdom terrified Mademoiselle de Watteville.

"And what ought I to do now?" she asked after a pause.

"To repair your wrong-doing, you must ascertain its extent," said the Abbe.

"Well, I will write to the only man who can know anything of Albert's fate, Monsieur Leopold Hannequin, a notary in Paris, his friend since childhood."

"Write no more, unless to do honor to truth," said the Vicar-General. "Place the real and the false letters in my hands, confess everything in detail as though I were the keeper of your conscience, asking me how you may expiate your sins, and doing as I bid you. I shall see-- for, above all things, restore this unfortunate man to his innocence in the eyes of the woman he had made his divinity on earth. Though he has lost his happiness, Albert must still hope for justification."

Rosalie promised to obey the Abbe, hoping that the steps he might take would perhaps end in bringing Albert back to her.

Not long after Mademoiselle de Watteville's confession a clerk came to Besancon from Monsieur Leopold Hannequin, armed with a power of attorney from Albert; he called first on Monsieur Girardet, begging his assistance in selling the house belonging to Monsieur Savaron. The attorney undertook to do this out of friendship for Albert. The clerk from Paris sold the furniture, and with the proceeds could repay some money owed by Savaron to Girardet, who on the occasion of his inexplicable departure had lent him five thousand francs while undertaking to collect his assets. When Girardet asked what had become of the handsome and noble pleader, to whom he had been so much attached, the clerk replied that no one knew but his master, and that the notary had seemed greatly distressed by the contents of the last letter he had received from Monsieur Albert de Savarus.

On hearing this, the Vicar-General wrote to Leopold. This was the
worthy notary's reply:--

"To Monsieur l'Abbe de Grancey,
   Vicar-General of the Diocese of Besancon.

"PARIS.

"Alas, monsieur, it is in nobody's power to restore Albert to the
life of the world; he has renounced it. He is a novice in the
monastery of the Grand Chartreuse near Grenoble. You know, better
than I who have but just learned it, that on the threshold of that
cloister everything dies. Albert, foreseeing that I should go to
him, placed the General of the Order between my utmost efforts and
himself. I know his noble soul well enough to be sure that he is
the victim of some odious plot unknown to us; but everything is at
an end. The Duchesse d'Argaiolo, now Duchesse de Rhetore, seems to
me to have carried severity to an extreme. At Belgirate, which she
had left when Albert flew thither, she had left instructions
leading him to believe that she was living in London. From London
Albert went in search of her to Naples, and from Naples to Rome,
where she was now engaged to the Duc de Rhetore. When Albert
succeeded in seeing Madame d'Argaiolo, at Florence, it was at the
ceremony of her marriage.

"Our poor friend swooned in the church, and even when he was in
danger of death he could never obtain any explanation from this
woman, who must have had I know not what in her heart. For seven
months Albert had traveled in pursuit of a cruel creature who
thought it sport to escape him; he knew not where or how to catch
her.

"I saw him on his way through Paris; and if you had seen him, as I did, you would have felt that not a word might be spoken about the Duchess, at the risk of bringing on an attack which might have wrecked his reason. If he had known what his crime was, he might have found means to justify himself; but being falsely accused of being married!--what could he do? Albert is dead, quite dead to the world. He longed for rest; let us hope that the deep silence and prayer into which he has thrown himself may give him happiness in another guise. You, monsieur, who have known him, must greatly pity him; and pity his friends also.

"Yours, etc."

As soon as he received this letter the good Vicar-General wrote to the General of the Carthusian order, and this was the letter he received from Albert Savarus:--

"Brother Albert to Monsieur l'Abbe de Grancey,
    Vicar-General of the Diocese of Besancon.

"LA GRANDE CHARTREUSE.

"I recognized your tender soul, dear and well-beloved Vicar-General, and your still youthful heart, in all that the reverend Father General of our Order has just told me. You have understood the only wish that lurks in the depths of my heart so far as the things of the world are concerned--to get justice done to my feelings by her who has treated me so badly! But before leaving me at liberty to avail myself of your offer, the General wanted to know that my vocation was sincere; he was so kind as to tell me his idea, on finding that I was determined to preserve absolute silence on this point. If I had yielded to the temptation to rehabilitate the man of the world, the friar would have been rejected by this monastery. Grace has certainly done her work, but, though short, the struggle was not the less keen or the less painful. Is not this enough to show you that I could never return to the world?

"Hence my forgiveness, which you ask for the author of so much woe, is entire and without a thought of vindictiveness. I will pray to God to forgive that young lady as I forgive her, and as I shall beseech Him to give Madame de Rhetore a life of happiness. Ah! whether it be death, or the obstinate hand of a young girl madly bent on being loved, or one of the blows ascribed to chance, must we not all obey God? Sorrow in some souls makes a vast void through which the Divine Voice rings. I learned too late the bearings of this life on that which awaits us; all in me is worn out; I could not serve in the ranks of the Church Militant, and I lay the remains of an almost extinct life at the foot of the altar.

"This is the last time I shall ever write. You alone, who loved me, and whom I loved so well, could make me break the law of oblivion I imposed on myself when I entered these headquarters of Saint Bruno, but you are always especially named in the prayers of

"BROTHER ALBERT.

"November 1836."

"Everything is for the best perhaps," thought the Abbe de Grancey.

When he showed this letter to Rosalie, who, with a pious impulse, kissed the lines which contained her forgiveness, he said to her:

"Well, now that he is lost to you, will you not be reconciled to your mother and marry the Comte de Soulas?"

"Only if Albert should order it," said she.

"But you see it is impossible to consult him. The General of the Order would not allow it."

"If I were to go to see him?"

"No Carthusian sees any visitor. Besides, no woman but the Queen of France may enter a Carthusian monastery," said the Abbe. "So you have no longer any excuse for not marrying young Monsieur de Soulas."

"I do not wish to destroy my mother's happiness," retorted Rosalie.

"Satan!" exclaimed the Vicar-General.

Towards the end of that winter the worthy Abbe de Grancey died. This good friend no longer stood between Madame de Watteville and her daughter, to soften the impact of those two iron wills.

The event he had foretold took place. In the month of August 1837 Madame de Watteville was married to Monsieur de Soulas in Paris, whither she went by Rosalie's advice, the girl making a show of kindness and sweetness to her mother. Madame de Watteville believed in this affection on the part of her daughter, who simply desired to go to Paris to give herself the luxury of a bitter revenge; she thought of nothing but avenging Savarus by torturing her rival.

Mademoiselle de Watteville had been declared legally of age; she was, in fact, not far from one-and-twenty. Her mother, to settle with her finally, had resigned her claims on les Rouxey, and the daughter had signed a release for all the inheritance of the Baron de Watteville. Rosalie encouraged her mother to marry the Comte de Soulas and settle all her own fortune on him.

"Let us each be perfectly free," she said.

Madame de Soulas, who had been uneasy as to her daughter's intentions, was touched by this liberality, and made her a present of six thousand francs a year in the funds as conscience money. As the Comtesse de Soulas had an income of forty-eight thousand francs from her own lands, and was quite incapable of alienating them in order to diminish Rosalie's share, Mademoiselle de Watteville was still a fortune to marry, of eighteen hundred thousand francs; les Rouxey, with the Baron's additions, and certain improvements, might yield twenty thousand francs a year, besides the value of the house, rents, and preserves. So Rosalie and her mother, who soon adopted the Paris style and fashions, easily obtained introductions to the best society. The golden key--eighteen hundred thousand francs-- embroidered on Mademoiselle de Watteville's stomacher, did more for the Comtesse de Soulas than her pretensions *a la* de Rupt, her inappropriate pride, or even her rather distant great connections.

In the month of February 1838 Rosalie, who was eagerly courted by many young men, achieved the purpose which had brought her to Paris. This was to meet the Duchesse de Rhetore, to see this wonderful woman, and to overwhelm her with perennial remorse. Rosalie gave herself up to the most bewildering elegance and vanities in order to face the Duchess on an equal footing.

They first met at a ball given annually after 1830 for the benefit of the pensioners on the old Civil List. A young man, prompted by

Rosalie, pointed her out to the Duchess, saying:

"There is a very remarkable young person, a strong-minded young lady too! She drove a clever man into a monastery--the Grand Chartreuse--a man of immense capabilities, Albert de Savarus, whose career she wrecked. She is Mademoiselle de Watteville, the famous Besancon heiress----"

The Duchess turned pale. Rosalie's eyes met hers with one of those flashes which, between woman and woman, are more fatal than the pistol shots of a duel. Francesca Soderini, who had suspected that Albert might be innocent, hastily quitted the ballroom, leaving the speaker at his wits' end to guess what terrible blow he had inflicted on the beautiful Duchesse de Rhetore.

"If you want to hear more about Albert, come to the Opera ball on Tuesday with a marigold in your hand."

This anonymous note, sent by Rosalie to the Duchess, brought the unhappy Italian to the ball, where Mademoiselle de Watteville placed in her hand all Albert's letters, with that written to Leopold Hannequin by the Vicar-General, and the notary's reply, and even that in which she had written her confession to the Abbe de Grancey.

"I do not choose to be the only sufferer," she said to her rival, "for one has been as ruthless as the other."

After enjoying the dismay stamped on the Duchess' beautiful face, Rosalie went away; she went out no more, and returned to Besancon with her mother.

Mademoiselle de Watteville, who lived alone on her estate of les Rouxey, riding, hunting, refusing two or three offers a year, going to Besancon four or five times in the course of the winter, and busying herself with improving her land, was regarded as a very eccentric personage. She was one of the celebrities of the Eastern provinces.

Madame de Soulas has two children, a boy and a girl, and she has grown younger; but Monsieur de Soulas has aged a good deal.

"My fortune has cost me dear," said he to young Chavoncourt. "Really to know a bigot it is unfortunately necessary to marry her!"

Mademoiselle de Watteville behaves in the most extraordinary manner. "She has vagaries," people say. Every year she goes to gaze at the walls of the Grande Chartreuse. Perhaps she dreams of imitating her grand-uncle by forcing the walls of the monastery to find a husband, as Watteville broke through those of his monastery to recover his liberty.

She left Besancon in 1841, intending, it was said, to get married; but the real reason of this expedition is still unknown, for she returned home in a state which forbids her ever appearing in society again. By one of those chances of which the Abbe de Grancey had spoken, she happened to be on the Loire in a steamboat of which the boiler burst. Mademoiselle de Watteville was so severely injured that she lost her right arm and her left leg; her face is marked with fearful scars, which have bereft her of her beauty; her health, cruelly upset, leaves her few days free from suffering. In short, she now never leaves the Chartreuse of les Rouxey, where she leads a life wholly devoted to religious practices.

PARIS, May 1842.

The Codes Of Hammurabi And Moses
W. W. Davies

QTY

The discovery of the Hammurabi Code is one of the greatest achievements of archaeology, and is of paramount interest, not only to the student of the Bible, but also to all those interested in ancient history...

Religion   **ISBN:** *1-59462-338-4*   **Pages:132**
MSRP $12.95

The Theory of Moral Sentiments
Adam Smith

QTY

This work from 1749. contains original theories of conscience amd moral judgment and it is the foundation for systemof morals.

Philosophy **ISBN:** *1-59462-777-0*   **Pages:536**
MSRP $19.95

Jessica's First Prayer
Hesba Stretton

QTY

In a screened and secluded corner of one of the many railway-bridges which span the streets of London there could be seen a few years ago, from five o'clock every morning until half past eight, a tidily set-out coffee-stall, consisting of a trestle and board, upon which stood two large tin cans, with a small fire of charcoal burning under each so as to keep the coffee boiling during the early hours of the morning when the work-people were thronging into the city on their way to their daily toil...

Childrens   **ISBN:** *1-59462-373-2*   **Pages:84**
MSRP $9.95

My Life and Work
Henry Ford

QTY

Henry Ford revolutionized the world with his implementation of mass production for the Model T automobile. Gain valuable business insight into his life and work with his own auto-biography... "We have only started on our development of our country we have not as yet, with all our talk of wonderful progress, done more than scratch the surface. The progress has been wonderful enough but..."

Biographies/   **ISBN:** *1-59462-198-5*   **Pages:300**
MSRP $21.95

The Art of Cross-Examination
Francis Wellman

I presume it is the experience of every author, after his first book is published upon an important subject, to be almost overwhelmed with a wealth of ideas and illustrations which could readily have been included in his book, and which to his own mind, at least, seem to make a second edition inevitable. Such certainly was the case with me; and when the first edition had reached its sixth impression in five months, I rejoiced to learn that it seemed to my publishers that the book had met with a sufficiently favorable reception to justify a second and considerably enlarged edition. ..

Pages:412

Reference   **ISBN:** *1-59462-647-2*   *MSRP $19.95*

QTY

On the Duty of Civil Disobedience
Henry David Thoreau

Thoreau wrote his famous essay, On the Duty of Civil Disobedience, as a protest against an unjust but popular war and the immoral but popular institution of slave-owning. He did more than write—he declined to pay his taxes, and was hauled off to gaol in consequence. Who can say how much this refusal of his hastened the end of the war and of slavery ?

Law   **ISBN:** *1-59462-747-9*

Pages:48

MSRP $7.45

QTY

Dream Psychology Psychoanalysis for Beginners
Sigmund Freud

Sigmund Freud, born Sigismund Schlomo Freud (May 6, 1856 - September 23, 1939), was a Jewish-Austrian neurologist and psychiatrist who co-founded the psychoanalytic school of psychology. Freud is best known for his theories of the unconscious mind, especially involving the mechanism of repression; his redefinition of sexual desire as mobile and directed towards a wide variety of objects; and his therapeutic techniques, especially his understanding of transference in the therapeutic relationship and the presumed value of dreams as sources of insight into unconscious desires.

Pages:196

Psychology   **ISBN:** *1-59462-905-6*   *MSRP $15.45*

QTY

The Miracle of Right Thought
Orison Swett Marden

Believe with all of your heart that you will do what you were made to do. When the mind has once formed the habit of holding cheerful, happy, prosperous pictures, it will not be easy to form the opposite habit. It does not matter how improbable or how far away this realization may see, or how dark the prospects may be, if we visualize them as best we can, as vividly as possible, hold tenaciously to them and vigorously struggle to attain them, they will gradually become actualized, realized in the life. But a desire, a longing without endeavor, a yearning abandoned or held indifferently will vanish without realization.

Pages:360

Self Help   **ISBN:** *1-59462-644-8*   *MSRP $25.45*

QTY

QTY

The Rosicrucian Cosmo-Conception Mystic Christianity by *Max Heindel*   ISBN: *1-59462-188-8*   **$38.95**
The Rosicrucian Cosmo-conception is not dogmatic, neither does it appeal to any other authority than the reason of the student. It is: not controversial, but is: sent forth in the, hope that it may help to clear...   New Age/Religion Pages 646

Abandonment To Divine Providence by *Jean-Pierre de Caussade*   ISBN: *1-59462-228-0*   **$25.95**
"The Rev. Jean Pierre de Caussade was one of the most remarkable spiritual writers of the Society of Jesus in France in the 18th Century. His death took place at Toulouse in 1751. His works have gone through many editions and have been republished...   Inspirational/Religion Pages 400

Mental Chemistry by *Charles Haanel*   ISBN: *1-59462-192-6*   **$23.95**
Mental Chemistry allows the change of material conditions by combining and appropriately utilizing the power of the mind. Much like applied chemistry creates something new and unique out of careful combinations of chemicals the mastery of mental chemistry...   New Age Pages 354

The Letters of Robert Browning and Elizabeth Barret Barrett 1845-1846 vol II   ISBN: *1-59462-193-4*   **$35.95**
by *Robert Browning* and *Elizabeth Barrett*   Biographies Pages 596

Gleanings In Genesis (volume I) by *Arthur W. Pink*   ISBN: *1-59462-130-6*   **$27.45**
Appropriately has Genesis been termed "the seed plot of the Bible" for in it we have, in germ form, almost all of the great doctrines which are afterwards fully developed in the books of Scripture which follow...   Religion/Inspirational Pages 420

The Master Key by *L. W. de Laurence*   ISBN: *1-59462-001-6*   **$30.95**
In no branch of human knowledge has there been a more lively increase of the spirit of research during the past few years than in the study of Psychology, Concentration and Mental Discipline. The requests for authentic lessons in Thought Control, Mental Discipline and...   New Age/Business Pages 422

The Lesser Key Of Solomon Goetia by *L. W. de Laurence*   ISBN: *1-59462-092-X*   **$9.95**
This translation of the first book of the "Lernegton" which is now for the first time made accessible to students of Talismanic Magic was done, after careful collation and edition, from numerous Ancient Manuscripts in Hebrew, Latin, and French...   New Age/Occult Pages 92

Rubaiyat Of Omar Khayyam by *Edward Fitzgerald*   ISBN: *1-59462-332-5*   **$13.95**
Edward Fitzgerald, whom the world has already learned, in spite of his own efforts to remain within the shadow of anonymity, to look upon as one of the rarest poets of the century, was born at Bredfield, in Suffolk, on the 31st of March, 1809. He was the third son of John Purcell...   Music Pages 172

Ancient Law by *Henry Maine*   ISBN: *1-59462-128-4*   **$29.95**
The chief object of the following pages is to indicate some of the earliest ideas of mankind, as they are reflected in Ancient Law, and to point out the relation of those ideas to modern thought.   Religion/History Pages 452

Far-Away Stories by *William J. Locke*   ISBN: *1-59462-129-2*   **$19.45**
"Good wine needs no bush, but a collection of mixed vintages does. And this book is just such a collection. Some of the stories I do not want to remain buried for ever in the museum files of dead magazine-numbers an author's not unpardonable vanity..."   Fiction Pages 272

Life of David Crockett by *David Crockett*   ISBN: *1-59462-250-7*   **$27.45**
"Colonel David Crockett was one of the most remarkable men of the times in which he lived. Born in humble life, but gifted with a strong will, indomitable courage, and unremitting perseverance...   Biographies/New Age Pages 424

Lip-Reading by *Edward Nitchie*   ISBN: *1-59462-206-X*   **$25.95**
Edward B. Nitchie, founder of the New York School for the Hard of Hearing, now the Nitchie School of Lip-Reading, Inc, wrote "LIP-READING Principles and Practice". The development and perfecting of this meritorious work on lip-reading was an undertaking...   How-to Pages 400

A Handbook of Suggestive Therapeutics, Applied Hypnotism, Psychic Science   ISBN: *1-59462-214-0*   **$24.95**
by *Henry Munro*   Health/New Age/Health/Self-help Pages 376

A Doll's House: and Two Other Plays by *Henrik Ibsen*   ISBN: *1-59462-112-8*   **$19.95**
Henrik Ibsen created this classic when in revolutionary 1848 Rome. Introducing some striking concepts in playwriting for the realist genre, this play has been studied the world over.   Fiction/Classics/Plays 308

The Light of Asia by *sir Edwin Arnold*   ISBN: *1-59462-204-3*   **$13.95**
In this poetic masterpiece, Edwin Arnold describes the life and teachings of Buddha. The man who was to become known as Buddha to the world was born as Prince Gautama of India but he rejected the worldly riches and abandoned the reigns of power when...   Religion/History/Biographies Pages 170

The Complete Works of Guy de Maupassant by *Guy de Maupassant*   ISBN: *1-59462-157-8*   **$16.95**
"For days and days, nights and nights, I had dreamed of that first kiss which was to consecrate our engagement, and I knew not on what spot I should put my lips..."   Fiction/Classics Pages 240

The Art of Cross-Examination by *Francis L. Wellman*   ISBN: *1-59462-309-0*   **$26.95**
Written by a renowned trial lawyer, Wellman imparts his experience and uses case studies to explain how to use psychology to extract desired information through questioning.   How-to/Science/Reference Pages 408

Answered or Unanswered? by *Louisa Vaughan*   ISBN: *1-59462-248-5*   **$10.95**
Miracles of Faith in China   Religion Pages 112

The Edinburgh Lectures on Mental Science (1909) by *Thomas*   ISBN: *1-59462-008-3*   **$11.95**
This book contains the substance of a course of lectures recently given by the writer in the Queen Street Hall, Edinburgh. Its purpose is to indicate the Natural Principles governing the relation between Mental Action and Material Conditions...   New Age/Psychology Pages 148

Ayesha by *H. Rider Haggard*   ISBN: *1-59462-301-5*   **$24.95**
Verily and indeed it is the unexpected that happens! Probably if there was one person upon the earth from whom the Editor of this, and of a certain previous history, did not expect to hear again...   Classics Pages 380

Ayala's Angel by *Anthony Trollope*   ISBN: *1-59462-352-X*   **$29.95**
The two girls were both pretty, but Lucy who was twenty-one who supposed to be simple and comparatively unattractive, whereas Ayala was credited, as her Bombwhat romantic name might show, with poetic charm and a taste for romance. Ayala when her father died was nineteen...   Fiction Pages 484

The American Commonwealth by *James Bryce*   ISBN: *1-59462-286-8*   **$34.45**
An interpretation of American democratic political theory. It examines political mechanics and society from the perspective of Scotsman James Bryce   Politics Pages 572

Stories of the Pilgrims by *Margaret P. Pumphrey*   ISBN: *1-59462-116-0*   **$17.95**
This book explores pilgrims religious oppression in England as well as their escape to Holland and eventual crossing to America on the Mayflower, and their early days in New England...   History Pages 268

www.bookjungle.com *email: sales@bookjungle.com fax: 630-214-0564 mail: Book Jungle PO Box 2226 Champaign, IL 61825*

QTY

The Fasting Cure *by Sinclair Upton*   ISBN: *1-59462-222-1*   **$13.95**
In the Cosmopolitan Magazine for May, 1910, and in the Contemporary Review (London) for April, 1910, I published an article dealing with my experiences in fasting. I have written a great many magazine articles, but never one which attracted so much attention... New Age/Self Help/Health Pages 164

Hebrew Astrology *by Sepharial*   ISBN: *1-59462-308-2*   **$13.45**
In these days of advanced thinking it is a matter of common observation that we have left many of the old landmarks behind and that we are now pressing forward to greater heights and to a wider horizon than that which represented the mind-content of our progenitors... Astrology Pages 144

Thought Vibration or The Law of Attraction in the Thought World   ISBN: *1-59462-127-6*   **$12.95**
by William Walker Atkinson   *Psychology/Religion Pages 144*

Optimism *by Helen Keller*   ISBN: *1-59462-108-X*   **$15.95**
Helen Keller was blind, deaf, and mute since 19 months old, yet famously learned how to overcome these handicaps, communicate with the world, and spread her lectures promoting optimism. An inspiring read for everyone... Biographies/Inspirational Pages 84

Sara Crewe *by Frances Burnett*   ISBN: *1-59462-360-0*   **$9.45**
In the first place, Miss Minchin lived in London. Her home was a large, dull, tall one, in a large, dull square, where all the houses were alike, and all the sparrows were alike, and where all the door-knockers made the same heavy sound... Childrens/Classic Pages 88

The Autobiography of Benjamin Franklin *by Benjamin Franklin*   ISBN: *1-59462-135-7*   **$24.95**
The Autobiography of Benjamin Franklin has probably been more extensively read than any other American historical work, and no other book of its kind has had such ups and downs of fortune. Franklin lived for many years in England, where he was agent... Biographies/History Pages 332

Name	
Email	
Telephone	
Address	
City, State ZIP	

☐ **Credit Card**   ☐ **Check / Money Order**

Credit Card Number	
Expiration Date	
Signature	

Please Mail to: Book Jungle
                                PO Box 2226
                                Champaign, IL 61825
   or Fax to: 630-214-0564

ORDERING INFORMATION

web*: www.bookjungle.com*
email*: sales@bookjungle.com*
fax*: 630-214-0564*
mail*: Book Jungle PO Box 2226 Champaign, IL 61825*
or PayPal *to sales@bookjungle.com*

Please contact us for bulk discounts

DIRECT-ORDER TERMS

**20% Discount if You Order
Two or More Books**
Free Domestic Shipping!
Accepted: Master Card, Visa,
Discover, American Express